of unique situations, or highlight specific traits in characters or a behavior that plays a key role in the story.

The imagery is brilliantly rendered in these collections. Listen to this: "Crissy had a way—a way of cutting, not like an attacker, more like a surgeon intent on removing what you yourself would agree is crimping you." Then in the gripping first-person narrative voice, a character describes the effect her husband's words have on the audience when he decides to break his silence: "My husband Carl is a man of few words until, in the rare moment, his words will burst into the atmosphere like a murmuration of starlings that assemble a fast-moving cloud and hijack everyone's attention." This is a collection of stories about human connection and Heefner is ingenious in his plotting, intelligent in exploring the human condition, and deft in weaving drama into the scenes. Fans of short stories will find it hard to let go of the characters in this book. They feel like people plucked from real life. The strong voices echo from these pages and the beautiful writing will keep you turning the pages. Unredeemable and Other Stories is a thing of rare beauty — each tale is engrossing and hard to part with.
— *The Book Commentary*

Dont Wake Me Fiction LLC

info@dontwakemefiction.com

Printed in the United States of America
First Edition: August 2023
ISBN: 979-8-218-26467-3
BISAC: FIC029000 FICTION / Short Stories (single author)

Front cover art by Dru Sumner.

Cover design by Bill Garrett.

Editorial Reviews

of *Unredeemable and other stories*

Sixteen stories illuminate the wonder of human connection in Heefner's collection.

To read this debut collection is to confront the messy, fragile, joyful business of being alive. "Everyone is their most interesting *while they're becoming* their best, not *after*," says the eponymous character in "What Crissy Calls Becoming," a wildly unpredictable story about a man who's unlucky in love, his new acquaintance, and the intense, more-than-friends/less-than-lovers relationship they develop. It is this "becoming" that unites the characters in these stories, a broad cast that hails from all over the map: They are from South Dakota and Oregon, Idaho and Kentucky; they are lawyers and store clerks, waitresses and car salesmen; they are children caring for their aging parents and divorced people looking to find love again, criminals on the run and spouses madly in love after years of marriage. All of them are searching for paths to their true and better selves. When an armed man threatens a cashier in "From Hibernation," Olaf can't help but intervene to protect his colleague—a heroic act that earns the attention of a local sheriff and threatens to expose Olaf's murky past. A recovering alcoholic in "Nosy SOB" becomes obsessed with the woman whose life he may have saved in a traffic accident, looking for ways to get in touch with her. "I Want To See Your Hand" follows Pam as she attempts to make amends with the woman her father unintentionally crippled years earlier. And in the title story, a tragedy at the Adult Sunday School sparks a man's heartbreaking journey to come to terms with his father's suicide. While the plots are sometimes overly intricate and hard to grasp, these stories reward a second read. The author writes with an impeccable eye for detail and endless reserves of warmth and humor—his sentences deftly capture the mundane and the sublime.

A lighthearted yet profound assemblage; every story here is a little miracle. — *Kirkus Reviews* (recipient of Kirkus Star)

★ ★ ★ ★ ★ | Reviewed by Romuald Dzemo

Unredeemable and Other Stories by Glen Heefner is a collection of short stories, a gorgeous offering that is resonant because the stories explore existential realities with characters that are memorable and hugely believable. For instance, readers will understand how the scars of youth shape the behavior and destiny of a man, how a man's consciousness of how little time he has left pushes him to rebuild his life, how a mother refuses to give up on a self-centered son, how a visit to an infant can change the life of a young boy. These stories feel like everyday experiences, but what makes them unique is the author's extraordinary ability to embellish the ordinary with insight, infuse life into seemingly mundane adventures, and make heroes of ordinary characters.

Human connection, the quest for meaning, survival, family, friendship, and love are some of the dominant themes in this collection. While each story is unique, Heefner succeeds to make readers get a strong sense of familiarity with the characters by permeating the stories with humanity and realism. Glen Heefner has a way with words and the terrific descriptions capture the nature of things, explore the beauty

Endorsements

Here are sixteen stories for the discerning reader. But be warned, this is not a book to sit down and read all at once as one might, for example, the collected works of Malamud or Cheever or Bellow, or even Faulkner, where one can read a half dozen stories and move on with life. These stories are *heavy*. They are filled with characters who are swept up in life's unpredictable ebb and flow, like people struggling against flood waters in the hope that what little they own still remains. And any reader worth his or her salt is immediately absorbed into each story. This can be exhausting.

The reason is Glen Heefner's exceptional writing talent, which grabs the reader and refuses to let go. The reader is sucked into the drama of everyday existence. And yes, it is exhausting—like being with a friend whose glass is half empty. You want to understand him but you can take him in only small doses. Otherwise, you find yourself spiraling into *his* oblivion. A writer who can make a reader feel that in a short story has exceptional skill.

Among these stories, I am partial to "They Mostly Have Faces." I was also captivated by "Nosy SOB," "Master of Quiescence," "Whose Will Be What," and "Rori's Words." That's not to say the remaining eleven stories lack the same strength and dynamics. It's just that these spoke loudest to me.

Not wanting to spoil a good story, especially a short story, by revealing too much about the piece, I do wish to address the key strength of each of these stories—character development. I'm amazed that Heefner can expose so much of a character's humanness, personality, quirks, prejudices, and internal struggles in so few pages. I'd compare his talent with Flannery O'Connor's brilliance in such stories as "A Good Man Is Hard To Find" and "Good Country People." Heefner matches O'Connor in the depth of human quirkiness and foibles. Throw in a compelling plot and how could you not want to submerge yourself into a captivating story?

As I mentioned at the beginning, this is a collection of stories for the discerning reader, one who understands the complexity and challenge of the short story genre, one who appreciates the sheer magic of a writer who can nimbly weave a story and hold your fascination the entire time.

—pdmac, former Creative Writing professor
and author of *The Wyvern Master Chronicles*,
the *Bridge Quest LitRPG* series, *Tombstone Trilogy*,
Beyond Her Touch, *Rebirth of Angels*, *Ctrl Z: The Do Over Stone*,
and the *Misfits of Gambria* series

These sixteen stories are unrelated—each told by a different voice about different people in a different place. But together they have a deep and powerful unity. Part of that unity is the intensity and detail with which those places are recreated, whether it is the voice and manner of a little girl with an injured dog, the littered space under rodeo bleachers where a long friendship is born, or the smell of an aging father's bedroom to a son who will care for him in his convalescence. Nothing is abstract here: each story immerses us, through all of our senses, in a fully-fleshed out world.

But the more important kind of unity is the insight that each story gives us into the mystery of being a self.

Many of them are about lonely people who long for, resist, and eventually accept companionship. The title story "Unredeemable" is a good example, beginning with the irony of its title. It describes a man who is a convinced unbeliever but a regular member of a Sunday school class. He is angered by the request to pray to a God in whom he does not believe for the recovery of the wife of a friend. But he nevertheless goes happily to a diner with the Sunday school class after the church service in which her recovery is announced. Currents of faith, doubt, longing, anger, and love circulate throughout this story. Your own personhood will be deepened by reading it, as it will by reading each of these stories.

—Dr. Loren Wilkinson, Professor Emeritus
of philosophy and interdisciplinary studies
Regent College, Vancouver, BC

Contents

Unredeemable
and other stories

What Crissy Calls Becoming

I had fallen on bad love luck, which I suppose any of us can. But the status of romance doesn't have to be an indicator for how well a man is doing, so I proceeded in character, without alarm, to live life as just myself. I was going out, damn it.

When the Bridger Range Rodeo opened its gate at 11:00, though, I was third in the general-public line, having been overzealous—having forgotten how much I don't like to be there for the pre-events nonsense.

It was important that no one peg me as freshly dumped, so I would keep my mouth shut. If you sit in the thirty-ninth row near the foul pole at Dodger Stadium, you just may be alone and invisible but, if you attempt this at the reach of the bleachers in most local rodeos, you will have company. Folks who settle into the neighboring seats will be grateful they don't have to stand, cheerful enough to insist on talking to you, and they will watch how you doff your hat for the anthem and they will ask about your father and mother and your brothers and sisters even if, like me, you don't have any. They will want you to reassure them, at least by your expressions, that they are okay and then they will always look like they're reserving the flippin' right to decide whether you are.

What Crissy Calls Becoming

On this particular morning, these intrusions felt in my gut like a poison, so I climbed all the way down and made for the vendor stands to get a dog and a Pepsi, to wash the bad feeling out of my system. But mid-transaction at the counter, a dizziness struck and dispatched me to the fence, where I shoved my fingers through the chain-link to do what I do so well about anything upsetting—pretend it away.

"They won't let me order till you pay," a large, flowing woman hollered in my direction, "and I'm diabetic, so just do me a little favor and let me know whether I'm going to die here." She was by my guess a couple years older than me, upper thirties. She came and stood squared to where I was.

"I just need a break," I said.

"Look, I'll pay for yours if you want, I don't care, but I have to tell them: are you gonna want your food or do I have 'em pitch it?"

My mind was barely there, looking around for my body. Then, as if I were in a black-and-white movie, and the director was coaching me with waves and whispers, I heard *Release your grip on the fence. Amble toward her. Pinch the sleeve of her windbreaker.* I had to assure her I understood and do this one good thing at least.

I waited for her, and we sauntered toward the crowd. We began to distinguish words in the hoopla from the PA.

My new acquaintance said, "You don't like the opening ceremonies."

"Says who?"

"Anyone who isn't blind."

"All right," I fessed. "They're like political rallies. I'm not here to see clowns and emcees flap their jaws, or listen to guffaws from stupid, prejudiced old people."

"I wouldn't have put it quite that way," she said, "but yeah, that's the way I feel too."

"It's bullshit."

She giggled.

We sat in the grit under the bleachers to ingest our snacks, to repair ourselves. She kept moving by little bits closer. I wasn't getting rattled at that. I realized we had needed to be closer to hear each other above the occasional roars of the crowd.

Her name was Cristina Cisneros, "but my friends call me Crissy." She asked me, "Why the rodeo?" I told her it was normal for me to come to these. "Normal or usual? Usual is what you do. Normal is how you feel about what you do, right?" She loved the calf roping. Why not steer wrestling? "Everyone is their most interesting *while they're becoming* their best, not *after*. I mean, the calf ropers, someday most of them will be steer wrestlers but, for now, they just keep steadily improving themselves, don't they. And what about you? Are you becoming your best?"

I flicked my cigarette away nearer to her than my earlier one.

My trick wasn't lost on Crissy. "So I'm making you nervous. I can read faces," she said. She had an easy pride. "Hey, if this feels too pointed, you can tell me your name. See, then I can say: Well Tom, are *you* your own best yet? That would sound nicer."

"It's Ray. Ray Ehrends."

"Oh my God, and you're running from a few friendly questions. I think I'll call you Running Ehrends."

The audacity I put up with that morning, and afternoon too, I would never have from a girlfriend. But Crissy had a way—a way of cutting, not like an attacker, more like a surgeon intent on removing what you yourself would agree is crimping you. That's why I let time get away from us, although she did later say she felt bad I'd missed my favorite segment, always the first event, the barrel racing.

"Why do you like barrel racing so much?" she had asked.

"It breaks my heart," I told her. "When I imagine the relationship between the horse and the girl, how they talk to each other. The men's events are about dominance, Man Over Beast. Barrel racing is about the horse's desire to please the girl."

"Oh, do you have a lot to learn. What do you want?"

I said I was fine, not at all hungry anymore. How about her?

"No, what do you want to happen? Tomorrow. Next week, next month. You don't have to tell me today."

I didn't.

A day shy of three weeks later, she called. "Come to Livingston."

"I hate Livingston. I hate wind."

"It's not always windy here. Besides, I want you to come to my house, which just happens to be in Livingston, for a barbecue tomorrow afternoon. Friends. A married couple and a young guy who's a nurse practitioner. You can bring anybody."

At my conception thirty-five years ago, my concocters doubled the dose of the party gene. Whenever music and laughter beckon, I slip into the zombie line, eyes closed, arms out, and walk straight to it. So I gave her invitation some receptive thought. I had two new original songs I'd been anxious to try out on fresh ears. New songs, new strings. One day I would audition in the lounge at Big Sky. First, first, there was the business of finding out whether people listening would be able to hear what I hear. Could I pull them into what I'd created? I know how to observe this while I'm playing. Would they let go of what they were seeing—some bearded dude and his scuffed up guitar—and lose themselves into the feeling?

But the guitar case never left my truck that day. I had gone around to the front to get it while the others were stoking the campfire, and Crissy followed me because the married couple were tangled in some of their own homemade tension while the kid nurse kept trying so poorly to shift their focus from that shit.

Right away Crissy noticed my new tires all the way around, raised whites, stunning underneath my cherry-red Ram. She rubbed her palm on the front one, back and forth, the way a window washer polishes out his final streaks. Her eyeballs rose and her lids fluttered. "I believe there's a story here," she said. She had to have been reading my face again, because indeed there was a story. The tires were new that morning. I'd got them on the Crow Rez for thirty bucks each, installed; no fees, no taxes. No guilt, despite there was plenty of cause for some. "Are you going to tell it to me?"

The sensation of having a ghost following me was strong, except that, instead of my being able to see through the ghost, this ghost was seeing through me.

"Hmph," she hummed, and gave the sidewall one more wipe. Then she bit her lip and in a choreographed-looking twirl flew around the side of her house, back toward the fire. And my inspiration to play the songs got sucked away in her draft.

Though the drive home from her house is easy and fairly short, the events—not of this barbecue day but of the first, at the rodeo—replayed to me. We were still under the bleachers when a uniformed officer asked had we seen a lost little girl. We hadn't.

Crissy faded to pallor. "We lost my sister when she was seven and I was ten."

"Aw…Crissy…what did she die from?"

"My sister didn't die. We really lost her. I could tell you where we were and what time it was and what the weather was like and why nothing we did that day or any day after ever mattered once we figured out she was gone. Everything changed. Things that mean the world to you can have no value the next week. Sometimes this happens in a minute."

I wasn't sure I could earn a place in this conversation, where trying was going to be important but you have to try the right way. Like in high school baseball, when Coach Bibbs explained soft hands and wouldn't stop hitting me grounders until I began *absorbing* those. *Okay Ehrends,* he said, *it sucks you were trying too hard. Tell you what—I'll keep in mind you care, if you'll remember fielding is a dance, not a schoolyard fight.* Crissy's story was going to be like one sizzling groundball after another, with some hops the in-between kind, but I was in. "Don't stop," I said.

"At first we were the three of us, fighting to find our fourth. We did the Amber thing, the police reports, FBI, the media. But when you're so close to the interstate, time is everything. We retraced our steps in that convenience store, scanning for clues *up, down, all around*, as Dad said to, always as the three of us. But eventually—and especially because there became less and less to do—even though we said we would never give up looking and hoping, guess what we did. Thing is, I started to realize…they had their way of missing her and I had mine. Whatever I would do from that time forward, I would do alone, and my sister, who had always been the only one who could have kept me from being alone in a case like that, wasn't there of course."

"Somehow you can tell this story to me and you're not crying, which means you've sort of moved on, doesn't it?"

"Tell you how." Crissy clutched my shoulder like a quarterback giving a blocking assignment. She kicked the dirt. That's how sobering this was going to get. "She was smart. So now I doubled my time on homework. I'd replace their smart daughter. Get it?"

"And all that busywork helped get your mind off the tragedy?" I may have been getting the hang of trying in the right way.

"It could have, Ray, I suppose, but it didn't. I cried more, actually. Nonstop. I went to the library and studied and cried. I checked out books on my subjects and I cried while they were stamping the cards. I cried in my classes. None of that made sense because my parents were already starting to feel other things. They were happy to have a smart daughter like they would have had. And I thought I was doing this all along for them, so their joy really should've pleased me."

A rock skipped only an arm's length from hitting Crissy. On the path that led from the vendors, there was an old crusty cowboy who'd rolled it our way. Then he yelled to us, "Y'all're missin' it!"

"Rent some teeth," I hollered, and I waved him off rudely but, on further thought, flipped him off and felt no shame. I could give Crissy back my eyes.

"One day in Physics, I had just answered a question right—about spring force—and it hit me. See, what I had always thought was, since she wasn't here, it was my duty to do things she would have done. That day I looked around and saw all the other smart kids nodding and it made me think, *Smart people are a dime a dozen.* What had made my kid sister special, unique in fact, was that she *saw* things."

I had the urge to ask what, but the story was at crescendo. I stuffed the hand I was going to use for emphasis back into my jacket pocket.

Crissy was pulling up anchor. Her head was reaching back. Whatever came out now was going to be straight from her past, not filtered by her present with me. "She saw my mom's moods coming when I didn't. She saw that Uncle Francisco, before he had said anything to anyone— even to my aunt?—that he'd gotten promoted to foreman. Well, she didn't know the job title, but she said *You're gonna boss people.* She heard it in the way he was talking louder to us. Ray, she knew that Milli, the lady next door, was pregnant with her second before Milli knew. Oh, that was awkward, until we all found out it was true. The little girl paid attention."

"I'm missing something." I hated admitting this. "How this ties into crying all the time?"

"The mad rush was over. The papers, the tests." Crissy punched the air. "The *surge* to get admitted to college, the part-time job…these I kept up, but I didn't feel detached, alone, like someone cobbling something together in a closet. Not anymore. The tears stopped. And I didn't have to march my accomplishments out in front of people to make the case that I love my parents. If you have to try to show you love someone, then maybe you don't. I could take the best of my sister and live that. I only had to open my eyes and let everyone's little signals in."

"They always give signals." Maybe they did. I was playing along, trying.

"Everyone does."

I let this settle. Crissy should have been ragged by now. Her voice should have gone breathy, her eyes puffy; she should have sighed and let her shoulders droop. No, she looked energized. Here had come the saddest of stories: shock, grief, resolve—what a plot—ending in the undoing realization that all of her trying, across years, had been misdirected. Still, as the story spilled out to me, or toward me, it had a stage presence, an alluring dignity, the way a professionally articulated sad, sad blues song does, if only for having been told so damned well. If you can describe your own misery to a T, can that get you to hope a little bit?

I wanted to know one thing more. "She's what, twenty-five years older now? Ever thought whether you might be able to recognize her?"

Crissy looked stumped by the prospect.

I grabbed her hand with both of mine and pulled her toward the path. "Let's go up," I whispered.

After the barbecue day, we maintained contact: calls, emails, texts; not frequent, not especially infrequent; never one-sided, never invasive. I had a couple of ex-girlfriends who had not learned this art, who I always wished had. In fact, it struck me one day that Crissy would have been an ideal ex-girlfriend, that I should consider looking for these qualities in my next girlfriend so that she'll already have those when she becomes my ex. But that's not what I did.

I did satisfy a long-held wish, though, when I started dating Gina: she was from *outside* my circle. She wasn't a friend of a friend, wasn't from work, wasn't crazy about the same types of music I was. She was fussy about what she ate; and she hated anyone smoking. So Gina was a true foreigner to me. And if things progressed, that would have to be because we wanted to be near each other's souls, not because we were too comfortable to move on. I liked the way she washed her bicycle once a week, whether she'd ridden it or not. She liked the artwork on my walls. These were the kinds of affections I had wanted: genuine, yes, but also unexpected.

We had some trip-ups, but who doesn't, I thought. At some point I noticed I'd never had the desire or even the thought to tell Crissy about any of those snags, so for all Crissy knew, Gina was a sprite, and my dalliance with her had been blessed in the skies. Still I'm sure that, when Crissy invited me to bring Gina on the camping trip, it had zero to do with any impressions I may have given her of Gina. Crissy was that way. She didn't have to like you. I'm not sure she had liked me at the rodeo. One day, I would find out what she saw in me—other than a prospective project.

The tents and cooking stuff and luggage amounted to only partly filling the wayback of the married couple's big conversion van. Settling into it felt electric, like our anticipation was streaming into us from an outlet under our seat. The Bickerers from cookout day were sitting in front. Crissy and the kid nurse were behind them, and Gina and I had the slight bit of backseat privacy the others were trying to give us on the way up. But, for whatever reasons, Gina kept addressing everyone from back there anyway. *Is that Ross Peak? You ought to be able to point your phone at it and see the name of it. Is there an app for that? Anyone want some raisins? Hey, how long have you guys had this van?* Eventually, Crissy rotated her captain seat around with a Tarot deck in one hand and her green vegetable grog mercifully enshrouded by the frosted plastic mug in the other.

"Okay," she said. "You can't ask me are you going to marry each other or how many children are you going to have, or how long you'll live. Cards or palms?"

I told her I didn't want to play. "Seriously, do Raj. Do Ellen…do Reese."

"I'm doing you, Ray."

Gina flipped her legs, parallel like in skiing, several times side to side. Those tan thighs reaching out from her khaki shorts looked awfully good doing it. My cheerful girlfriend had embarked, with me, on a camping adventure from the edge of the great valley floor.

I took this to mean *Who cares, Ray? Let Crissy entertain us for a while.*

Crissy overturned the cards, one by one, and laid them out in several strips with overlaps. She used her thumb and index finger to keep sliding them by tiny amounts, at times back and forth, not at all repositioning them, rather being contemplative, not strategic. At last she looked up. "An elderly man will come into your life. He is not currently in your life, do you understand? This man will assist you in some way." She rested her elbow on her knee, squeezed her forehead. "I'm seeing a little bit of guilt…No, it's not necessarily guilt. Regret is what I can say. It's not big, but it's in there. Now. Maybe this man is going to help you to let go of that." She started to pick up the cards, stopped and clinked her top and bottom teeth together. "And there's some kind of animal you don't have yet. It's not a dog."

"I don't get why you guys think this is fun," I said. "I told you to do Raj."

It was a few weeks before Christmas. I got the only distress call ever from Crissy. She had been shopping in Bozeman and dropped a figurine, a crystal skier she was thinking about buying for me. When she'd started to totter, she instinctively opened both hands to soften her landing on the tiles. Someone "very smart and kind" noticed her alert bracelet and ran like a gazelle to buy her two bottles of juice at the food court.

"I'm all done resting now, but can you pick me up? I'm in the hospital on the east side here and I need a ride back to the mall to get my car. They brought me here in a meat wagon."

She was only four or five miles away and out of danger, as she had said, but I shook. I propelled the Ram without wits or peripheral vision toward the ER, nearly scraped a Miata on the way.

"What?" she said, when they let me through the curtain. "You look so scared. I told you I'm fine."

As we picked through a little traffic, I told her what a privilege it was for me to have been the one she called.

"Stop. Stop," she said. "No, not the car. Stop talking and listen…Yes, I could have died today. I wasn't all that close to dying, but it made me think of things I need to clear up. One of those has to do with you, Ray. There is no elderly man. There is no animal that's not a dog."

"You did a *new* reading for me."

"No, dear. I don't read cards. I messed with you. You were the only one in the van who didn't have a future. I mean, of course you have one, it's just that you don't see one. The rest of us do. You don't have a picture of anything that isn't now. Well, you say you want to do things, but you never do them. And why, Ray? I thought if I made things up, then you would see *something*. Then something of your own would come into view. The fact is…you're still drifting. You let life blow you around like the Livingston wind."

I couldn't think.

"Now I'm asking you again, Ray. What do you want?"

Gina broke up with me in April. Now my thoughts were on having been the victim of a doomed relationship, not on having lost her. But a sadness was, after all, seeping into all the little things I did every day. The unfairness was like an itch I couldn't scratch enough. The Bickerers were still together, reportedly doing better, speaking softer words and laughing, and they had been breathing the same air Gina and I had here in the Gallatin valley. I would wake in the middle of the night realizing I'd been having a conversation with myself, more like I'd been testifying, really, responding to questions that the other me was asking. Although this was extremely uncomfortable, in the end it seemed to yield something. I was not one bit closer to figuring out what had been going wrong in my love life, but my yearning took a shape.

If I had angels, they were Crissy—for sure—and my neighbor Jonesy and his girlfriend, and just by virtue of the other guy's seeming to be always around during the intervals when I needed people around, our aloof landlord too. The property was our one-lane road in the foothills, with our three houses on the one side and the vacant wooded tract on the other, where, throughout my years there, we would occasionally throw a night fire in the pit and talk and talk. I was now coming to see that they were excellent companions. Several times they had asked me to run inside and grab a book and read them a short story in the flickering light. After the reading, I would stand up a little woozy from having entered the story and then having been reluctant to come back to my own life, and I'd set another log on the fire. I hadn't ever thought of these times as building memories and certainly not as a chance to swap visions. I'd only seen it as passing time and burning through some downed wood to keep the piles from getting unmanageable.

One of the stories I read to them involved a man whose car hit another that had pulled out in front of his. The collision dealt serious injuries to the driver of that other car. The protagonist fully understood the accident wasn't his fault, but he too was damaged. The following weekend Jonesy said he really liked the one about the accident. Reflexively I corrected him. "It's not about an accident. It's about a man who doesn't know what to do with his remorse over something that wasn't his fault." When Jonesy looked confused, I said, "The things that move us the most are not the events in our lives. They're what we can and can't do when those events happen." He said he wanted to think about this, and that particular story never did come up again between us.

This morning I was drying my hair when Jonesy called, frantic. He was still in bed and had woken to a duck flying around his bedroom ceiling, bumping its breast against the walls like a cue ball, he said, and sometimes slapping its wings against the blades of the idle fan up there. Could I come over? *Now.*

I shot out my door and into his house, hushed once I got in. On a big old Pioneer speaker in the little living room was a male mallard, rigid as a statue. The duck allowed me to walk straight to him, cup him between my palms, and carry him outside, where I set him on the grass and dropped my arms.

He was hard to read at first, not like a human whose eyes tell all, but I did read him. There he stood for at least six full seconds, I think more like eight, free but not moving.

Then he soared over my head and Jonesy's roof to where I couldn't see him anymore.

Tonight Crissy called. She said there was news, news that I should hear as soon as possible. She had seen the Michael Atkinson lithograph I'd given Gina for Christmas, had seen it advertised for sale on Etsy. This is the sort of thing no one wants to tell you and only someone who deeply cares would let herself be the one to.

"How do you know it's the same piece?" I asked her.

"How many *gdabernathys* do you know?"

I heard me breathe out, like preemptively purging myself of something. "Crissy, look. Thanks. I understand why you're telling me this. We can talk later."

"Cool. I really gotta go eat something right now or I'm in big trouble! Call me whenever."

I sat at the laptop to bring up Gina's Facebook page and find out whether she was mentioning the Atkinson. Maybe to see her latest pictures, her latest friends. Maybe I wanted to find out how sorry I should feel for myself or how relieved I ought to be to not have her anymore. I got lost in her page. By the time my phone announced that a text came in, nothing had crystallized, but I had a general feeling of preparedness, similar to the sense of impending wellness you have when a dose of medication you just started taking has almost kicked in.

I'm still staring at her page, though, the same way that duck this morning kept staring at me. He certainly did. He was locked up inside himself. For all that time. Before he came to understand he was free.

But that's it, isn't it? "Alexa…Play R-E-O Speedwagon It's Time for Me to Fly."

From Hibernation

In a perfect world a store like the U-Do-It would hire separate staff for closing hour. These special people would hustle the restocking cart down the aisles to home in on the correct tiny label and slide the item back into its place, all through the miracle of the twenty-twenty vision they were hired with. And they wouldn't be six-foot-six. And no one would take their perfectly good name like Olaf—even if it is his contrived and temporary alias—and call them *Oaf*.

But every night Olaf would stoop and kneel and then spread his sore knees to get that much lower, splaying his 15-EEs across the aisle, all the while expecting a last-minute shopper's cart to roll up behind him and ring out its metallic Excuse Me Please. He would bow to the shelf and run his neck out and back to where the final distance made the fuzzy dots on the shelf labels morph into letters and digits. Maybe, only maybe, one set of these was a dead-on match for the alphanumerics on the box that the earlier customer flat out neglected to put back.

If an hour began with forty in the cart, he had a minute-and-a-half per item. More than once he had thought that Lester—Lester Mailey, his boss—figured this is a classic job for the patient and meticulous guy he can call Oaf. And more than once of course, Olaf pictured himself pushing that cart all the way down to and right on into Mailey's office and whispering to him, *U-Do-It*.

A jing-jing interrupted his concentration. It was the cart of the requisite late shopper, who at least had the decency to say "Hi" before expecting Olaf to yield the aisle. The programmable light switch timer in Olaf's hand was a match for a label, so he gave it back to the shelf.

"Yes sir, just one second," Olaf said, and ground his knuckles against the tile to drive his massive chest forward and give his legs the space to straighten up on the toes of the *hippos*, which is what Mailey had taken to calling Olaf's work shoes.

"It's OK, I've got time," the customer answered, "if you're not trying to close early."

Now standing, Olaf was towering over the gentleman, whose tight grin might have been dorkish in a sports bar but was winsome in this moment at the U-Do-It. "You'll find what you need tonight. I promise," Olaf said.

The little man held up a muddy GFI outlet from a free-standing outdoor circuit that had likely been feeding a fountain pump, and he pointed Olaf's eyes to a sheared-off plastic pipe lodged in its mounting threads.

"You beheaded your fountain outlet?" Olaf asked him.

"Well, I'm a violent person. I'm Dean," the little man said, leaning in to get a read on the badge. "You're Olaf?" He stuck out his hand, which charmed Olaf enough to slap his own into it.

"Let's get that box first," Olaf said, "then we'll see about the whole violence thing." A half dozen absurdly long strides and Olaf pulled up, turned to Dean. Said in a hush, "Now be extra quiet. These outlets can sense danger."

Dean chortled so unexpectedly that he had to wipe his nose with the back of his hand. But Dean's grin fell and his forehead wrinkled and an instant later, no, first, yes first, a scream louder than the Tuesday morning siren test resounded from the front wall of the store.

Olaf's soles hovered as the hippos came about. His hands shot to the center of the aisle, where the right grabbed Dean's cart and the left flattened against Dean's chest. Olaf shucked these squarely against the shelf wall as the hippos launched him like a rocket up-aisle, from where he knew he would burst to, scope out, and then own the entire front of the store.

As he reached *The Promenade*—Aisle 1, Brillo—Becca the cashier cut loose another scream, this one higher and weaker, and now he could see her and her arm was bleeding. People were running. Mailey was running! Customers were dropping behind pallet stock like prairie dogs on rewind. Some guy was even running past Olaf and that made no sense. Olaf slammed on the hippo brakes, spun from left, where Becca was, to right, where the hell-bent guy was making for the near door.

Olaf gained an instant bead on the runner. This was going to be too easy. He immediately began outpacing the man. At the consummate instant, calculated fifty times in the five strides he had taken, Olaf dove and hooked his palm against the top of the runner's boot. Step One complete.

Step Two was to spin both himself and by extension the other guy one full barber-pole twist before they each landed face down on the tile, where this collision was announced by what sounded like a china teapot exploding inside a dish towel. And Olaf thought, *That just could be the bastard's cheekbone.*

Michelle had left a half bottle of wine and a half glass of it on the counter, not for Beau and not even deliberately, he supposed. The only way to reconstruct this is that she'd been restless, and the romance movie was so boring she barely made it to bed. Next to these was a four-by-six sheet of note paper folded into a tent, with only MTDW (empty the dishwasher) in severely left-leaning block letters and the outline of a heart superimposed.

Three years earlier they had wed, surrounded by debutantes in Charleston, and then honeymooned as inseparable tourists in Savannah. When she'd said, "Y'know what'd be perfect is if we skipped out to Cumberland Island and stalked those wild horses," Beau checked the weather page, plotted the ferry departure, made it all happen. He had dived into his marriage headlong. On this night, with his chair only half pulled up to the tiny kitchen table, he resigned to a pang, that the closeness he needed would not come until morning; and that this feeling, even in the ideal marriage, is similar to the gnaw of lonesomeness.

But a sweet sound like a song, "I think you're maybe late," echoed from the narrow hallway of the bedroom. "You're not tryin' out for manager, are you?"

Beau tapped his fingertips on the kitty-corner seat. "I have to talk. Wanna wait till morning? I mean, it's not life or death. It'll keep, Chelle, really."

She has something she does when she wants to act cute-surprised, a thing he'd never seen any other woman do. She lays her fingers on her cheek, wipes it front-to-back in a single, very snappy motion, and finally then does what others do: opens her mouth and slaps her cheek. He wonders every time, *Where did the first step—the wiping motion—come from?*

Beau once saw part of a movie involving a particular old couple. The man was out clearing a long driveway with a snow blower. He muscled the big machine around and whoa—his wife was standing there holding out a steaming mug. To look at her, you saw she had just a knitted shawl around her shoulders and only house slippers on her feet, so her bare ankles were in the snow. This wasn't a pivotal point in the film but recorded itself in Beau's head because Michelle breaks his heart like that, that's the kind of thing she would do. Two years ago on his birthday, she kicked the wooden screen door open and took his blazing cake out onto the back landing. She held it under the soffit and sang Happy Birthday through the screen, the entire stanza, herself under a heavy downpour. "I thought it would be more meaningful this way," she said on her way back in.

When Beau jerked the drawer open to grab a handful of dish towels for her hair, his dad seized onto his forearm and said, "The Good Lord'll b'stow this on only just a few." Out of respect, Beau faced him to nod, but Dad finished, "I ain't congratulatin' *you*, y' damned fool. Gold is gold." And so she was, indeed, this drowned rat who adored him beyond sensibility; she was gold.

Michelle's eyes are a smidgen too far apart for the absolute comfort of an observer. In fact she isn't cross-eyed, but it took Beau some studying to conclude this when they first met. Otherwise she is of ordinary features on an ordinary frame. Her dishwater blonde hair is in two asymmetrical waves toward the back that ultimately fall to just above her shoulders. It's drab enough that in low light it can make you wonder whether it's gray. And God cleverly designed this ordinary package to camouflage the gem, her smile. But then everywhere she goes she blows the secret, letting everyone see that smile, making everyone melt.

"I think I'm getting used to Oregon," she said, "so don't tell me your important thing is for us to move again."

"It's not about moving. It's about our cover here, though. I might've blown it."

"We can talk now if you want, but first do something for me. Lose that stupid badge off your pocket?" She grimaced, and squinted like a TSA agent till he dropped the U-Do-It Olaf ID face-down on the table. "Thanks. You know how much I hate that thing. All right. I saw Elton John this afternoon. He said he'll be history by some time tomorrow. But let me tell you, he's one unhappy camper about moving."

Justin Ville was the real name of the guy across from them. Beau often said it's uncanny how much he looked like a young Elton John, big glasses and all. Despite that they and Justin had the only houses around, they didn't know him well. The only thing they had in common with the guy was they each had that short walk up their lane to fetch their mail from their boxes at the highway, and they never even brought one another's back. But, yeah, Beau thought, they did know a few things. "I thought he *wanted* out of here," Beau said. "It was even his idea. I know I'm remembering this right."

"No, Sweetheart. Well, OK, I was generalizing. He does wanna go but, my God, does that man hate packing. Yeah, he's cool with leaving to go to work for his brother. Anyway…let's talk about you, buddy. You look so mopey. What do you say, come to bed now and I'll make you a nice gam sandwich."

"When did you start with the wine, and I'm only—"A percussive *CRUMPF* from outside toward the highway got them checking each other to see how they should react, whether to run out and make sure everything is okay or continue talking, which is what Beau—wary of his impulses on this snakebitten night—finally did. He supposed, "Elton John ran over his own realtor's sign. No, wait. He hit his head on his open trunk door, loading up the car. So…when he closed it, he taught it a lesson."

"Or it's Mrs. Plum in the Lounge with the Candlestick," Michelle countered, and pinched Beau's ear because that was all the grip she would need to pull him to the bedroom.

Exactly what the sheriff wanted to dig further into was the million-dollar question. And speaking of dollars, Beau felt *Mailey had better be paying for this early Monday start*. Beau had the coffee mug by its girth instead of the handle. The hot was numbing his fingers, but that felt oddly right. Sometimes—is it when you're a bit nervous?—you're just more comfortable being a little bit uncomfortable. He had tried to focus on the Seahawks team championship picture and also snooped at the family photos on the desk, where Mailey had the lenses of his reading glasses precariously balanced on the frame that holds the daughter's picture. The pale yellow walls enclosing the office of this man who owned *a flippin' paint department under the same roof* may have been the distraction that was constricting Beau's throat. He was parched, like he had been eating chalk dust. Friday night's interview with the sheriff had been unremarkable, with questions like *Who is Dean?* and *What's Dean's last name?* and *How did you know the running guy was the one who hurt the cashier?* But there were two others that made Beau concentrate on not fidgeting: *You say you lived in Bend before moving here?* and *Is this a southern accent I'm detecting?*

Possibly this second meeting would be nothing more than an admonishment on what constitutes excessive force, how the threshold is lower for liability than for violating the law. The guy with the broken cheekbone might sue. He could contend that if Beau had said *Stop sir, please come back here*, then he The Bastard would have cheerfully halted, turned around and dropped the knife, and presented his hands in the universal cuff-me position. Beau knew from Prelaw all about liability, so he had to remember to put an *Oh, really?* on his face if the sheriff tried to explain it.

But the sheriff didn't. "I need you to help me, Olaf. You were a hero last Friday. Let's see if you can be a hero today. I've got to figure out why a guy…buys a van with cash in Gainesville, Florida and then rents a house on the west slope of the Cascades six days later. Take your time. You want a topper on that coffee?"

Beau made a gentle bite on his lower lip before realizing he had. He thought back to debating in college, specifically the trick to not blushing, to picture in this case the sheriff in boxer shorts. Now Beau was ready. "Why does a robber go to Gardening, grab a pair of gloves, go to Hardware, put on those gloves," Beau was counting these actions out on his fingers while reciting, "and grab a new Stanley knife before going to Checkout to do a holdup? Why not bring those props in with him? Those things wouldn't be bulky enough that the Service desk would notice."

"Let me tell you how this works, Hero. I look into everything." The sheriff used the back of his forearm to push Mailey's binder and sat one thigh on the desk, blocking about a fourth of Mailey from Beau's view. "We can do this at the justice center," he said, "if you'd be more comfortable there."

Beau took a deliberative pause. "Some people buy…a *better* car before cruising across the whole country. You know, over those mountains with their best belongings."

"That's my line," the sheriff said, grinning. "*I've* told *you* that's what our hero had done. Your job is to fill in why. And on the subject of your job," at this he looked over his shoulder to Mailey, "Les, I have no doubt you'll be dealing with at least a false identity here. Aliases are legal, but so is firing somebody who didn't reveal all of theirs. So Olaf, did you meet my deputy Friday night? Red hair, wispy goatee? He's questioning Michelle right now."

Beau's phone was half out before he released his clutch on it and let it slip back into his pocket.

"That's all right. These devices really are something, aren't they? I love this thing," the sheriff said, flaunting his iPad. "This is a free country. 'Course, if you do pull out your phone, you'll find out how free this country is for somebody in *my* position. Which reminds me…do you want an attorney? If you've broken a law, any law, you're gonna get Miranda. Now, both of you were Poli Sci, according to Michelle," he said, looking down at his iPad, "so I don't need to explain what Miranda is before I read it to you. How about it?"

Beau slapped his knees and did a slow shake of the head in spans that diminished until it stopped wagging. He looked through his lashes, up at the sheriff first, then at Mailey, and opened up, *game over*. "We're not running from the law. We're running from the press."

The sheriff's thumb wedged under his waistband and he used a flick of the head to tell Mailey to leave for a while. When the door closed, Beau heard for the first time ever how quiet it is in that office. With their move from the East now exposed, it dawned on him that the peace he had craved Friday night in his own kitchen could be within reach, so he laid out the story.

Yes, they were Poli Sci grads. They were extraordinary talent, ripe for any of several campaigns, on the stipulation that whoever took one of them had to take the other. They got hired for the governor's race in South Carolina, home state for both. Michelle's specialties were formulating arguments and counter-narratives, deciding when to release information, coaching debate practice sessions. His was research: excavating dirt to soil the opponent and extracting factoids that would polish his guy's image to an impervious shine.

"When we were eight points up, everything was fine; better than fine, considering we had great software and deep funding. When it went to a four-point race, things got dirty.

From Hibernation

We needed an issue to stump on, and the campaign determined that Immigration should be it, which may've been fine in itself. But the top people wanted to point the press to examples that coincided with our guy's speeches about protecting Carolinians from these *invaders*. Let's call that dirty. Somebody got the idea, *Wouldn't it be opportune if some Latino kid in Columbia*—our capitol, not the oil and coffee nation—*got caught taking a pistol to his mostly white church?* So it got dirtier. But to make that happen, you need quiet people who know other quiet people to select the kid to corrupt. At the same time…you need clandestine people who know scummy people to get a gun, the right gun. And you need other clandestine people who know other scummy people to put the gun into the kid's hands. You even need someone to start the rumor at the church on that day. Nobody was supposed to get shot, much less a couple of kids. But you had to have ammunition in the weapon. This is all documented by now, and neither of us was implicated and both of us cooperated with the investigation."

The sheriff rolled his hand, like *Don't stop. Don't even breathe.*

"We didn't know this was going on. We did know something was. The managers were behaving like I expect they would if layoffs were coming. There were doors closing. They stopped asking about our projects. In fact Michelle was convinced we were gonna get let go. Anyway, what they did was *wrong*, and neither of us would've stayed in the campaign if we had an idea what they were doing."

"But you sold out the managers, right? Because they were *scraps*? Remember Friday when I asked did you want to know the perp's condition, and you said, *No, that's just scraps.*"

"Oh, no, I told you, neither of us ever knew about the plot, let alone the underworld part. Pfff. Dusey. Our D-Line coach in college? I was right defensive end. One time I blew up a screen left, their tight was in a heap. I was standing over the guy to see how bad it was. Dusey ran halfway across the field at me—and that's something because he was a load—anyway he was screaming, *That's scraps! Leave it!* Well, in the locker room later he says, *When you finish a great meal, it wrecks the aftertaste if you sit there starin' at the scraps.* No, Michelle and I didn't rat anybody out because we didn't know anything. We told the investigators about the edginess, how the office had changed and nobody cared about my stats or Michelle's fishbone diagrams all of a sudden."

"And the running here, to Oregon?"

Michelle and Beau had talked plenty about pulling up stakes. He explained, if he'd been a *scientific* researcher— "This is an example," Beau said—and some scandal ruined his project, he could've been hired right away into a different project on the strength of his credentials. But scandals in politics take no prisoners. "No other campaign is going to touch you because someday the press will recognize your name and call it out, and the opponent will use that to render your candidate dubious. We couldn't *permanently* change our names, because we'd never be able to flaunt our degrees and honors again. But if we went undercover for…a couple years, we figured—which ought to be long enough for the most sinister journalists to stop wondering what we're up to——we could eventually get picked up by another campaign. Say, one in a different region. Like here."

The sheriff pushed himself to his feet. "Let me get Mailey for this next matter." He summoned Mailey by phone, turned back to Beau. "I'm gonna check all this out. I've got a way in mind that the press won't see, but I'll need you to cooperate. Give me the names of a few people who questioned you guys and cleared you. My wife's an administrator for the high school, you see, and she can make those calls. She can say she needs two History teachers, that you told her everything when she interviewed the two of you for jobs, and she wants to make sure it's all true. These investigators, they wouldn't know whether either of you is certified to teach?"

Beau pursed his lips, shook his head, *No*.

"See, here in Oregon, there's reciprocity, meaning…if you were certified in South Carolina, you're good-to-go here. The things you learn at the dinner table if you keep your ears open when your wife rambles." The sheriff's smile spread and seemed to hold while Beau recalled a profusion of dormant detail.

When Mailey re-entered, the sheriff suggested to him, *You might be interested in this next part*. "Now, Olaf, what's your name?"

"It's T-H-I-E-R-R-Y, pronounced like I have a theory, first name Beau, B-E-A-U. Lester, I'm sorry. I'm from South Carolina, not Bend. God, I am truly sorry I wasn't forthcoming. And I'm not sorry like I'm trying to keep my job; if you want me to go, I'll go. I'm sorry that this wasn't fair to you. See, I thought I had…well, if you're interested in keeping me, please talk to the sheriff. He's gonna check me out thoroughly."

Mailey nodded but didn't betray what he was thinking.

The sheriff headed to the door, scrolling his iPad as he walked. Halfway through it he pivoted. "The first time you met your wife…why did you tell her your name was Nat Turner?"

"What? Are you kidding?" Beau said. "All right. Saturday morning I told her what happened here Friday, and I said, 'I'm afraid you're married to Nat Turner.' The man was a slave. We're both familiar with his story. He led a rebellion that freed about a hundred slaves, partly by murdering white owners. He hid for a couple months, but *he didn't leave the county!* They found him and the story gets much uglier. No, I never used that as an alias. You get it, don't you? I was *free* of all that stuff in Carolina, *we* were free, and then I had this…grand reaction, I guess, intervening Friday and now my cover, our cover, is blown. Michelle must've got cut off explaining. Who knows. I don't know."

The sheriff rubbed his ear lobe and grunted over his shoulder. "Les, I'll see you. Mr. Thierry, I can't order you, but let me encourage you not to move again any time soon."

One of the coaches in the Seahawks photo looked to be picking his nose. Not yet off the hook with his boss, Beau thought better about pointing this out to Mailey, who was sweeping his notebook back with the meaty part of his hand.

"There's a ton of floor units to put together in Lighting," Mailey muttered. With a nakedly thespian pomp he softly pounded his desk and was obviously pleased his reading glasses feared him; they chattered against the top of his daughter's frame. The gesture did fail so miserably though that, for the second time in about a minute, Beau needed to chomp on his lips to fight back a perilous guffaw. "But for now, the cedar two-by is a holy mess. It'll take a big Oaf a good couple hours to restack. Out to the yard, okay? Man, are we behind. Man."

The damp highway hissed against Beau's tires the whole sixteen miles home where, under the front light, the mist was suspending itself. The hippos hydroplaned a bit on the flagstone but that made easier Beau's jig to undercut a slug and sling it behind him onto the gravel lane. For the first time in their nine months here, Beau didn't feel like an outsider. The jamb stop released the front door with its familiar disgruntled cracking sound, but the growl was this time pleasing to his ear. How hard they had worked to be completely at home here, and to remain unremarkable and unknown. But oh, how liberating the latest turn of events might just prove to have been.

On the kitchen table was a four-by-six paper tent that said

> *I told the deputy everything. I knew you would*
> *tell the sheriff the truth. We will never flounder*
> *as long as we have each other. Wake me up.*
> *—Mrs. Thierry*

There was a trim patch of hair sketched into the V of the M in *Mrs.* This note was headed for the archives, the collection at the bottom of Beau's socks drawer, the modest stack that also had the one that said *I do I do I do.*

Even felons appreciate a sense of relief after coming clean, Beau supposed, and some of them keep that sense of ease for months or years, but although the Thierrys each consciously poured encouragement upon the other in the week that followed their coming out, still Michelle in particular tended to a kind of despair. In quick order she went from scribbling journal entries and sketching elaborate garden layouts to the pronouncement *This is not home.*

By Thursday morning the sheriff's wife had concluded her phone chats with the Carolina investigators. They had been generally friendly to her questions. Although the whole case was closed, the detectives still had recollections of the innocent. Also, the deputy had finished his own background checks on the Thierrys. So the sheriff let them know these things in a terse call to their home number, the one registered to Olaf. Terse perhaps because Michelle put him on speaker so Beau would be part of the conversation, or terse because *that's just how he is or that's just how sheriffs are.* But instead of riding this acknowledgement well into the new day, Michelle within a half hour was ready for a full pardon from their *self-sequestered bullcrap extended second honeymoon* and was demanding to have back the near year they had lost to it.

"I'm in atrophy here in Bedford Falls," she said, referring to her part-time office work for the small plumbing firm run by George Blele, which rhymes with Bailey.

"C'mon, you've got prestige. You're married to the foremost authority on why diagonal pliers are no longer displayed on end caps."

"I should be getting a pedicure right now and sippin' a mint julep."

"Why can't you be happy for *me?*" Beau argued. "I mean, I'm the all-pro defensive end for the Nobody Nothings."

Things are especially unsettling whenever Michelle altogether stops. This time it made Beau yearn for the complaints he tried so hard to stem only a minute ago. He winged one more remedy, "Well, I'm still the best damned grocery shopper of all the men in this room, so get me your list."

"I'm coming with you," Michelle said. "It's coupon time. Did you bring the paper in?"

Beau did the spin he'd invented, an about-face maneuver that shows obedience while making light of the tone of voice that got him moving in the first place. Michelle's face held back expression, but her belly under the silk nightie detectably vibrated with the giggle she was suppressing.

By the time the jamb stop let out its second *CRRR-ACK*, she was already in the kitchen *bra-ed up*, as Beau would say, and pulling her pale green knit top to her waist. He wiped his shoes several times on the mat just inside the door.

"It's raining again?" she wondered.

"It's Admirably Dewey. Now check this—we got a nice little letter here with no nice little signature." He handed her the sheet, a plain eight-and-a-half-by-eleven with what seemed to be Roman 12-point black, folded into thirds as if it had been intended for an envelope. It stated a brief sentiment:

I hope the two of you are very happy

"This was in the box?" she asked him.

"Yeah…no…not the mailbox, the newspaper box. Inside the paper, as a matter a fact." He spread the Valley Watchman open across the *dollhouse table*, as he had taken to calling it. He pointed to where he'd felt the letter through the first page, between **Lane Closures End Till Spring** and **Student Perishes After Rollover,** with the latter article's gnarly wreck photo.

"Cute note. So somebody loves us. Well, ain't that sweet?" Michelle is the rare person who can be sincerely charming while mocking something. "Oh, broccoli, as in let's get some," she said. "As in let's get a move on too."

Beau turned on his heels, that theatrical move, but stopped halfway through. Michelle added BROCCOLI to the list and twice tapped the top of her pen against the table, signifying that the imaginary timer for their errand had begun to tick. To drive the point deeper, she spoke, in that Carolina-bad British accent of hers, "Time waits for no one, Taplow."

"And so do I," said Beau, finishing the line from *The Browning Version*, then whispering something that included both "married to a cinephile" and "pain in the ass," but neither of these with heart.

Over the next two weeks, Beau hitched himself to her moods, watching for them and stepping as adeptly as he could in between Michelle and what was irritating her, but his pattern became obvious. Like anything obvious can, it became obnoxious too. So he stopped asking her to choose movies. And although she accused him of forgetting that she's trying to find a *real* job, he stopped turning the *Valley Watchman* to the **Help Wanted** section for her and in the latter week didn't even bring the paper in. When a new letter came tucked in the *Watchman*, Michelle had a whimsical thought Beau might have been planting these, just to stir things up. This one said

Nothing can interrupt your happiness there

That night when he got home, she was still up, and outright asked him did he write it, but he rifled back. "Are you losing it?"

"Then you tell me, what's *your* theory, Mr. Thierry," she said, playful with the name so Beau would understand she wasn't taunting him. "Maybe it's supposed to be like those signs your dad used to talk about. C'mon, Beau, from road trips, when you were little? Gillette."

"Oh, Burma-Shave."

"Yes. They would have signs that you have to add together to get the meaning? So let's put these two together."

"It's unnerving, Chelle. If this keeps up, we're gonna have to do something." So first he wouldn't run with her tease about him being the culprit, then he wouldn't laugh at her Burma-Shave notion, and now he went vague: *we're gonna have to do something*; meaning Michelle was going to have to.

"Oh, that's rich," she said, pulling the bottle from the fridge to refresh her wine glass. "So the plan is no plan."

"Well, you could talk to the paper boy next Thursday morning while I'm still in bed, if you can squeeze that into your busy part-time work schedule. Or better yet, call him Wednesday night when I'm at work."

"What's that gonna do, hotshot?" Michelle demanded to know. "You think that little kid and his mother—oh, here—his mom says, *Wait a second, honey. Don't put the paper in their box until I slip this spooky letter into it. OK, honey. Now jam it in there*" and on *jam*, Michelle drove her palm forward with teeth-clenched gusto and some hip. "I got an idea. You, big guy, you get out there and cut down that viburnum that's blocking our view of the paper box. Or is that too strenuous?"

"I'm not doing it." Beau cast an evil eye on her wine as she drew from the glass. "We are not re-landscaping the place we don't own, just to nab a prankster." He shook his head at the wine glass, so Michelle took a pretty good gulp from it, and Beau killed the discussion. "If it happens again, I'll talk to the sheriff."

And it did. Michelle had phoned the paper boy's house and spoken to him and his mother, who knew nothing and were put off by the questions. What Michelle didn't do, though, was get in front of the kitchen window to watch the paper-into-the-box process, which may have been a waste of time anyway since the viburnum really did block the view of the box, plus about three car-lengths of the roadway in front of it. But by the time she got the paper, a third letter was already in it.

And no WORLD OUT THERE for you two

Beau said not to touch the thing in case somebody will take fingerprints from it. He nudged it into a gallon baggie and put it next to his wool jacket on the arm of the couch by the door, where he already had the first two letters staged.

Before going to work, Beau walked the too-many short and wide steps up to the justice center, thinking, *This is like school: they wear you out getting there so you'll be ready to be taught a lesson inside.* He found himself electronically frisked like everyone. Then he was insulted by the sight of most others who also had business in that place, and was consciously annoyed by the echoes, all before pushing open the heavy door into his appointment with the dependably daunting sheriff.

"Your wife coming separately?" the sheriff asked, before Beau reached the guest chair.

"She's not coming. We sort of divided our duties around this."

"Then you divided mine. Thanks. You cut in half my ability to help you. Did you make that list of all persons who might wish to harm you or make you squirm?"

"It's up here," Beau said, pointing to his brain.

"Great. We need it out here," the sheriff said, making an umpire's home run circle with his index finger. "Did you bring the love notes?"

"Ah, the letters? Sure. There are three. These two are touched, but the one in plastic could have the fingerprints you'll be looking for."

"I'll be looking for likelihood—you know—motive, access. Here's a likelihood: it's likely that the perp's prints aren't logged anywhere, so we end up saying, *Oh, what a fine set of unidentifiable prints.* Still, this is going to be my deal, not yours, Hero. In a case of this kind, it's not likely the perpetrator is going to confront you in person, at least until it's time to make their final move. So don't sit on your front porch with a firearm. Now, play to likelihoods: who's your best guess?"

"Whenever we talk about it, we keep coming back to the guy who cut Becca at the U-Do-It, because he's got to be thinking he could've gotten away with the robbery if it wasn't for me."

"What about your old buddies in Carolina? Let's say one of them went down for his crime and figures one of you overheard him at the water cooler while he was planning the deed? Wanna broaden the scope a little?"

"Well, doesn't that person then single out me and not Michelle, or single out Michelle and not me? See, in your scenario, that person remembers *one of us* being at the water cooler."

The sheriff leaned on his elbows, hands folded under his chin. "Does she even know you're here?"

"Of course," Beau affirmed.

"Right. See, I made an assumption that she knows most of what's going on in your life. These Carolina suspects, they would think that too. So…you heard something and told her, or she heard something and told you, then you each told your interrogators. Revenge can take on strange forms but I'm telling you, harassment is one of them. Revenge starts with a plan, then always loses patience. It can go to threats and then violence, but it picks up speed as it goes. That's why I'm taking this seriously, and it would've been helpful if *both of you* did."

"But they're in jail."

"What was that word you used about their contacts? Under…something. Help me out here, sport. Underworld. People who aren't behind bars but do illegal things? Now, looking at other possibilities, yes, we do have the guy with the shattered face in custody, and maybe he has a friend do a favor, OK? Typing up a few intimidating notes? Thing is, the connection is so near that if this ties back to him, frightening a witness, he'll never get out. His lawyer would've warned him not to do anything stupid. But then again, revenge can be irrational."

"What do you think about a security camera?" Beau asked him. "Like, should I install one?"

"You might net yourself a nice quality picture of some vengeful person doing something horrible to you. For your photo album? Listen, it's good to think in very broad terms right now, be aware that it could be anybody. And talk to me. Is either of you having an affair?" the sheriff probed, but Beau dismissed this question with a scowl. "Could it be someone has a crush on one of you, a love interest you haven't been aware of? Just think about it, someone clingy, because then we're dealing with just an annoyance. But what's bothering me is this last one, *...no WORLD OUT THERE for you two*. The sarcasm is deeper, so it starts to feel like there's a threat. Have you thought about the wreck?"

Beau was stumped. "Neither of us has been in an accident."

"Not you," the sheriff said. "That night you got involved at the U-Do-It, maybe hour-and-a-half after that, you must've been back to your house by then. The young lady driving home from the junior college. Does this ring a bell? Do you guys read the paper? She ran off the road. We figure she swerved to avoid a deer, because the road was good and visibility was tops. Anyway, her SUV rolled over, and this was right there on the highway by where your little road spurs off. She would've been okay with her injuries, except under her left ear she had an awful laceration. Now, in any kind of a *multi-car* event, somebody calls it in and the paramedics get there. Mr. Thierry, that poor girl's car wasn't spotted in the brush until dawn Saturday. She bled to death. Right there, strung upside down by her seatbelt like a sparrow caught in a vine, only because nobody knew she was out there. Is any of this familiar?"

"I remember there was something in the paper about a student, yeah. A student fatality, but I didn't read the paper that week."

"Well, here's the thing. I went to the funeral, just to say on behalf of my guys how awful it is that nobody saw her car. The mother was...destroyed. The girl's dad wasn't even there, but he's alive somewhere. Two years ago he finished up the child support, so Mom hasn't heard from him. I did a little poking, talked to the girl's friends. She saw her dad from time to time, on her own, so he's probably not far away, but he's not in her cell phone. This guy's past is checkered with weapons and violence charges. Let's say he blames you and your wife because he can't see why you wouldn't have heard the crash and called 911. If I knew where he was, I'd have a deputy under cover sidle up to him in a bar."

After the meeting, on his way to work, Beau called from his car to see if he could get Michelle at George Blele's. She did pick up, and he told her about the accident.

"Chelle, think hard. Do you remember hearing a noise?" he said, already resolved not to ask her about any admirer.

Saturday morning in the cottage was always catch-up time. Not for just personal news, but also for doctoring wounds of the soul and patching dings in the young marriage. This day had those regular expectations, but also the anticipation of breakfast out, a table for two for the Thierrys—Michelle's idea, the best one Beau had heard all week.

While Michelle readied herself, Beau checked fluids in the truck and added a quart, which is why he was able to hear a car at some distance. When his oil slowed to drips, he sidestepped and looked behind himself. A weathered silver sedan was idling in front of Elton John's vacant house. A forty-something woman who must have driven it there was on foot, approaching Beau. She had outdated glasses on and a lightweight midnight-blue parka, hip length, so she was probably not a realtor; but her gait was steady, so she may have been. Beau gave her a warm greeting. "Hey, good mornin'."

This woman's squint, with her chin held high, looked almost like she was trying to see over the top of some obstruction. "I might be buying your neighbor's place," she said, "so I have a question for you both. It'll only take a minute."

Beau thought, *How the heck do you know there are two of us?* and then realized he had been chasing his wedding band up and down his ring finger with the oil rag. "Let me go get my wife," he told her.

Michelle was almost done. Beau explained what was going on and lobbied her to pause with the primping and get back to it after their maybe-new-neighbor leaves, but she fussed. "Why don't you go tell her whatever she wants to know, and then I'll come out and say *Hey*, and we'll leave."

But a scheme was on fire in Beau's hip pocket: to take Michelle to the animal pound after breakfast. He had seen a sign Thursday by the county complex, then bought a leash at the U-Do-It before clocking in. Today they would pick a dog she'd love and adopt it under the still-serviceable name

Olaf. Naturally first he'd address all things here, like the new neighbor lady, and then get back to keeping any telltale spring out of his steps. "Come hither, I *pray* thee," he bid his bride, offering his hand.

"Oh, yes, m'lord," she obliged, and slid her palm on his until her little hand was enveloped in it.

Beau led her through the narrow hall toward the front room-kitchen area. His shoulders almost spanned it and almost brushed the walls, so Michelle was like a coal car in a mine, tugged in lurches by the engine that will always tow it safely out to the airy daylight. Her hand pulsed. Squeezed is what it would have done, if possibly she could ever get her hand around his. Beau knew in this instant, no matter what happened in their life, they would always be together. And if there is an afterlife, they would be together in that one too. Not a word was spoken between them on the way to the front door, but he was certain Michelle was thinking, *My Beau, I will follow you anywhere.*

The buyer lady was still standing next to the viburnum. In fact, she may have not budged an inch in the several minutes Beau was inside.

"This is my wife Michelle. I'm sorry, I didn't catch your name. Anyway, Chelle, this good lady is considering buying Justin's house and she has a few questions."

"Only one," the woman said.

Backlight from the low sun to his left played in Michelle's hair. The breeze puffed through a patch of it that might have been the object of the grooming she'd felt was still left to do. But this imperfection was perfectly hers, the way a few bent feathers on a wing may make an angel irresistible.

"Sure," Michelle said, "let's hear your one question, 'cause Beau and I have a date. I'm sure you understand." Then she checked her husband, looking for him to agree, and realized he'd been staring at her. His attention to the present was clearly outrun by his affection for his wife, which he was wearing like a favorite hat.

The woman said, "So, you two have been…very happy here?" Now she had Beau's attention too. "You might think I want revenge. I did hate you, and those God-blessed pills were supposed to be helping. Well, the notes…that was selfish. All about me."

"Oh, ma'am, there's no need to apologize," Beau interjected. "We—"

"No. Let me finish. Those notes were all about *my* hurt, not truly for my daughter."

"We're so very sorry," Beau said, looking over his left shoulder to Michelle, anticipating she would nod and seeing she already did.

In his right ear he heard the woman's parka swish. Apparently she was stirring to leave. Then he heard, *My daughter only wants everything to be equal.* Still fixed on Michelle, he saw his bride gasp and whisper, "Sweet Jesus—." A burnt metallic scent reached him with a pop a whole second before Michelle crumbled, even before her slender right hand slipped from his.

But this is where Beau's recollection of the event fogs. He says he was aware of his arms hanging distended, as if his hands had been weights of considerable mass. He thought to act, of course, to trust instinct, but then to not. His heroics at the U-Do-It had revoked his privilege to be nimble in any instant.

He does remember his legs came unstuck first. He disarmed the woman. In fact, he broke her arm and he threw the pistol and her car keys into the weeds and strewed the contents of her purse all over the lawn. Then tore the pockets off her parka before he found her cell phone, which he used to call for help. He just doesn't remember how he synced these things with tending to Michelle. But while he held her in his forearms, he remembers screaming toward the woman, "Don't move an inch, and keep your fucking mouth shut! Please, ma'am!"

The woman's account remained consistent and was oddly uncontested from when she was taken into custody at the scene through the end of her trial and beyond. That she did not shoot to kill, she did not shoot to injure anyone. That she brandished the weapon and fired what she thought was a stray round. That what her daughter had wanted equal was the *terror* the couple would know at the *prospect* of death.

Michelle emerged on the other side of all this with some debilitating nerve damage to her left hand. She has never once blamed Beau or held it against him. If you carefully watched them, you would see no difference in the way they shower affection on each other. If you really trained your ear on them, you might detect that some of the music in Michelle's voice has flattened. But this could be only a side effect of her further maturity.

Only if you were Beau would you know a hollowness from time to time as you stand in your upscale Salem townhouse and look to the large dining table or the granite countertops or the swank nightstand, where the tent messages she no longer writes would have been delicately propped. *But she can let me hold that hand now*, you remind yourself, and a joy floods through you. *Forget the notes. Forget them*, same as you muttered the day you lit them, the day you set them all free. And that is how you still admonish yourself, whether you're in a mood to listen or not.

I Want to See Your Hand

In almost-summer of 1959, my two closest Downers Grove friends drifted. *Too busy, maybe tomorrow. Mom won't let me. That doesn't sound like fun. You're not the same.*

Oscar had been in charge of teaching me how to throw not like an eleven-year-old girl, which I incontrovertibly was. When we didn't have a baseball handy, a fallen apple was perfectly serviceable. To gird me for a long and pleasant life, he told me more than a few times that I should consider the bad boys, who had fireworks, dangerous. And that I should stop hating Mr. Pascoe, since I just might be able to learn something from that man if I could pretend the thick black hairs didn't stick quite so far out of his nose. Solid avuncular mentoring was this specialty I hoped Oscar would carry into his grown-up years. Seventy, like me, he would be now.

To Wendy had fallen the business of discussing, ad nauseam, the repugnant looming monthly cycles. For example, how to annotate the day on my calendar, which I would have to quietly purchase. You draw a lazy semicircle whose ends connect to the left edge of the day. Then the leg of the P is implied by the printed border between the days. *That's how my big sister does it. And you don't have a sister so you better listen to me.* She tried so hard to teach me how to weave pig tails and sew clothes together that I felt sorry for her until she gave up. Later, creeping toward adulthood and for all time since, I have often been vindicated by realizations that I shall forever be lost in the spatial world. Give me two dimensions and stop talking. I can handle those.

In recollection I blame my familial situation for Wendy's and Oscar's widening distance from me. If I had really begun to act differently toward them, I'll never know how. I know only when.

My husband set the glass of milk onto my placemat as he often does. Though so familiar, the act then—a few weeks ago—revealed an accomplished fact I hadn't considered for years: that Leo's hands are as strong and functional as they ever have been. Typically I would consider this an attribute to be credited to Leo, owing to the caution he always practiced in his work and personal life. But that morning I deemed it a blessing *afforded to* Leo, the gift of having been allowed to keep this that he was born with. Many men his age have failed to keep their hands intact.

What would he be like without this gift? What would this mundane sight at the kitchen table have been if the glass always came with two hands, one assisting the other?

What if one of these otherwise magnificent hands had been forever crippled, disconnected from all intelligence, by a single negligent act of someone else? What if this daily sight were relentlessly heartbreaking? I sprang to get an ancient clipping from the bottom of my underwear drawer.

We kids each were, by hastily scribbled individual notes, summoned home right after school, my older and younger brother and me. Then told to sit together in a row on the couch.

"No, not there. On the couch. Now." Mother pulled the rocker up. Father was busy in the garage, so he wouldn't be coming in. "You will each need to know this. Your father was at the filling station this morning. Someone in front of your father was backing up, so he did too. A lady walked behind our car. He didn't see her. The back bumper hit the lady in the leg."

Our own gray '52 Dodge?

"Her leg was severed below the knee, maybe when he hit her or maybe when he pulled forward after he did."

Tough guy Raymond demanded to know which filling station. Little Davey cried out, "Why didn't nobody yell for Daddy to stop?" I half-stood and threw up on the Persian rug. Davey ran to his room. Raymond yelled "Yuck!" and stiffly strutted out the front door. I sank to my knees and hovered above my mess.

"Pammy, you have got to be careful, yourself," Mother said. "I know you go there for Cokes sometimes. The lady was coming from the Coke machine."

"So what?"

"We know this because, when she was knocked down, the bottle broke and made a god-awful gash in the palm of her hand. They said she can't move that hand now."

"I can't be here," I told Mother. I couldn't.

What I could do, two days later, was forego my allowance-Twinkies at the Rexall in favor of a copy of the *Village Progress*, in which the article memorialized—for as long as I have kept it—both the mistake and its life-altering consequence upon the lady named Mary Lynn, exactly ten years older than me. Grown up, only barely. All but the color of her dress was noted. To this day I can't make it past the first three sentences but I will never discard it.

Let's all call it Mary Lynn's fault for buying a Coke. Mother left me with that impression whether she meant to or not. Mothers have to hold their families together. They can acknowledge that someone in the family has done a wrong thing but, boy, does it help their stance if a merely whimsical choice by the victim pitched in somehow toward the unthinkable result. If only *that woman* hadn't... I was lucky twelve years ago, a few minutes before Mother's last draw of breath, to assure her she had done right in the way she'd explained the accident. Lucky to be able to tell her that lie.

Leo and I drove to Dave's in St. Paul a few weeks ago for Thanksgiving, as we typically have done since we lost Raymond to lung cancer. I had never shown Dave the article or discussed it with him. To get some time alone with him was hard for me, as I knew it would be. Mainly, I wanted to find out whether he ever thinks of that woman. What would *he* say to her? Does it still bother him?

He took us down to a whisper, then talked about when Dad sold the car. "My baseball cards were under the back seat. That's where I kept them so nobody could steal them. I never knew he was trading in the Dodge. Think what those cards would be worth."

"For God's sake, David! What has become of you?"

"Not me. Not just me. Look Pam, Dad was never the same again, and Raymond—"

"Leave Raymond out of this."

"That's when he took up smoking, and you know it. And what about you? Remember Oscar? If you want to get all sanctimonious, leave me *out* of this."

"Do you ever think about the lady, that's all I want to know. I guess I have my answer."

"Get real, Pam. I'm just saying, we all lost something."

I turned my back on him, slammed the pantry door to leave him alone to stare at the cans and boxes. I couldn't help but hear him hurl one final, muffled remark, though.

"We did, Pam. All of us."

Leo says he understands. He might. He doesn't understand how I could have kept the clipping for nearly sixty years, or why. Around information, Leo is more a serpent than a coyote. He devours it with no thought of sharing. And once he has, he would prefer to abandon the bones instead of tuck them away.

He has found Mary Lynn for me. At the time of the accident, she was to report to a teaching job in Wisconsin the coming September. He said he used his connections to locate her in an independent living facility in Delavan. What connections I do not know, except that those are bones from which he has chosen to not walk away. I don't question him. He came home with not only the address and the fact that Mary Lynn had gone on to become a grade school principal in Delavan until she retired, but also train tickets between Downers and Chicago, and Chicago and Harvard. Cab rides will whisk me from Harvard to Delavan and back to Harvard, about twenty minutes each. I wanted to ask Leo, almost did, would he like to join me. But I saw. He had already spoken.

Still, I was not content for him to have dealt himself cleanly out of the picture, if that was what he was trying to do. I needed him. I needed him to try out my ideas and help me see what my visit would be like.

"Do you think I should bring her flowers?"

"No."

He crossed to his overcoat, pulled a fat paperback Alice Munro from the pocket, held it front-cover to me. "Four hours each way with all the deadheading. I thought about shorter stories, but you'll have plenty of time."

"Should I call her first?"

"And say what?"

Answers are so easy when there aren't any good ones. Husbands so fluidly shed their reluctance to weigh in.

Metra has been much more pleasantly distracting than driving with Leo could have been. From the very platform, it fixed me upon a scientific mystery. Why is there, mixed in with the pungent diesel exhaust, a distinctive odor of steel? This must mean that friction broadcasts some dust form of the steel into the atmosphere. An insignificant amount, to be sure, but a detectable amount, given that this septuagenarian has so readily concerned herself with it.

Mary Lynn was a teacher. A principal. There may have been a day when she too had this same sensation and was led to this same pondering about the railroad, which would have meant that—for however long—she had been freed from being mindful of her disabilities. Maybe of the attendant horror in it too.

Of course she had.

Hillside after hillside with its carved-out nook cradling another barn each composed one of the self-contained frames in what felt like a slideshow out the window on my cab ride up from Harvard. Most of those barns, I'm sure, were already standing sixty years ago when Mary Lynn experienced her maiden journey to Delavan and her first-ever solo teaching position. Never mind what grace the school board had promised her for accommodation. Never mind how deep and wide her academic credentials may have been. This Wisconsin, slide after pastoral slide, had been poised in *Hello*. Was she recognizing the salute?

On the house phone they slid to me, I told Mary Lynn I was Pamela Gianetta and that I was in the lobby to see her. Knowing nothing more than that, she said, "Oh fine, dear. I'll be right down. I'd say I'll be the one rolling toward you, but that won't help, I'm afraid. There's a lot of rolling going on in this place."

"I'm in a gray wool coat, knee length."

Knee length? Christ Above, what is wrong with me?

I have heard that it's all right to ask a blind person whether they *see* your point. It could be she's taken this remark as benign, taken it in stride. *Don't say in stride.*

And don't apologize, and don't apologize for your father, and don't ask whether she's comfortable. If she's not, she'll move. Leo was so good reminding me of certain thoughts to banish.

"Take the wing chair, Pamela. All my friends tell me it's the most comfortable. No, the Lady's chair, the wider one."

"Mary Lynn. I've brought you nothing, nothing but myself."

There's something little-girlish about her. It's around the nose and her forehead. At eighty. And she's going to let me talk, I can tell.

"Mary Lynn, I've come from Downers Grove. I am Earnest Sawyer's daughter."

She's leaving! She pushed the lever to turn right, to wheel her chair away. She's rolling, five feet or so, now ten, to capture one of the staff who's dashing by. She'll ask him to escort me to the door.

"Kevin, dear, would you be so kind as to bring a cup of coffee to my friend Pamela? And one to me."

Driving the chair back to face me, she pulls a few tissues from the box on the end table, hands them to me. She saw the glaze.

"Go on, dear. Kevin will be back pronto. He's so kind."

"If I've unsettled you—"

Mary Lynn brushes away the thought with a backhanded wave of her left forearm. This let me see a prominent scar on her palm.

"Oh, thank God. You're right-handed."

"No, I'm afraid I was born left-handed. I had to learn to write with my right hand." She laughs. "At first my signatures looked like forgeries," she laughs again, "but I never had to teach penmanship, so my credibility remained very much intact with the students. Until I turned them loose upon the world, of course. There are a few I still deny ever having known. Now, let me get to know you."

I don't get very far before Kevin whispers *Forgive me* as he slips between us to deliver the cups.

"There's something you should know, Pamela, in case you don't already. It was your father who took his belt off and used it as a tourniquet on my leg. The doctor said that saved my life. I didn't know who he was, I thought he may have been the manager at the Texaco. The insurance company told me much later who the man was. So! On behalf of all my wonderful students across my career, I say, Thank you."

I've been aware of a presence behind me. And now a dark-haired man's hand on the wing of my chair.

"Timothy, dear, this is my old friend Pamela. Please go to the desk and call a cab for her? She's got a train to meet. We'll be only about fifteen more minutes."

Timothy obeys.

"My son. They retire so early these days. Timothy can come over here almost at will. Oh! How I do *love* Alice Munro. You know, Ontario is quite similar to Wisconsin in many ways. I have another son as well. So sorry you won't be able to meet him."

The driver doesn't know Mary Lynn. I asked him, which makes it okay to call Leo from the cab to tell him about the visit.

"She says my father was the person who wrapped the tourniquet around her leg and saved her life."

"Hang on. I've got the article you left on my dresser. It's right here in front of me." There's a thin but palpable innocence in Leo's tone of voice all of a sudden, the kind I might hear if he were about to say, *I did eat ONE cookie but, Pam, it's the best cookie you ever made.* "Did she say what your dad had on?"

"No, only that for a long time she didn't know who he was, maybe the Texaco man."

"What was your father wearing?"

"A white shirt. That I know for sure. He always wore a white shirt to work. He was on his way to work."

"The article says a man in a blue shirt did that."

Oh, my God. Should I go back?

"Pam," Leo whispers, before I can ask, "come home."

Delavan and the countryside to its south are flashing by so much faster than on the way here. I think that's a good thing.

Take me, Alice, take me to Ontario.

A Mischievous Frolic in Beit Lekhem

Mother and Auntie have sent their little neighbor boy to bid that I visit them when finished, whenever I am content in preparation of my advocate pleadings for the morrow's docket. The hungry fig thief who foraged for his children's supper; the bedeviled soul whose wandering eye did linger, beyond reason, upon his neighbor's wife; she of nape browned by the afternoon at the market, the sun entitled to kiss her neck, the neighbor not entitled to leer at its handiwork. And the other fig thief, he more prolific, profoundly less defensible.

Justice is whatsoever the magistrate shall decide, not what is left to the reasonable mind, not what is hoped for. Thus attests the inscription on the imposing stone I set years ago behind me, binding myself to accept his judgment while I silently hope that some day a perceivable fairness will arise from it. This advocate's reminder that one does not both play in a game and adjudicate its outcome. My stone more subtly also suggests that my years of service have jaded me.

I shall walk to Auntie's, both hands wrapped round the second sash that drags my right foot behind my left. I will gush out my irrepressible love of them and trace my footprints back until I can drop into this night's dreams of the morrow's acquittals.

Justice is whatsoever the magistrate shall decide. This haunts me, though I am never at liberty to admit so. I focus on the craft. I must be a reader of events, see today what occurred yesterday. At my faltering, I will tell you that I can read nothing of the kind. At my most fortunate, indeed, I can read much. I have used this equivocating summary to convey, to my few young understudies, both my uncertainty and my faith. Two of them have confessed their desire to become *iuris consulti* whenever Rome may establish this profession as lawfully gainful. Verily I fear they will ever so gradually regard the art of persuasion less and less as they pursue the glory of scholarship. So I intend to admonish them against that.

For decades now, Mother has tried to weave what happened to my ankle to a foreboding I did not sense when fate had set itself to damage me. She knows—full well—I did not sense it, but she nevertheless imputes all guilt to me. No, this injury was wrought by only my ingenuous youth. When, whimpering and crippled, I awakened the house, I could not cloak my new impairment, but told her the goat had kicked me.

"You went to the stable, though you knew the infant was special in some way. You had no business there."

Mothers do this to you. "I knew nothing."

"You tempted fate, my son."

As I told their little neighbor to say I would, I have come to visit. Having witnessed my approach, Mother has barely kissed my cheek before starting again on how I suffer because of only my childhood indiscretion.

I tell her, "Do I not plead for others that it was only the aggregate weight of randomly converging factors *in a few seconds' time* that had wrinkled their sense of responsibility? That their weakness is a mere mark of the moment, not a trait that the guilty carries about or would ever boast of?"

But my facetious deflection has failed. I can read this, I will not tease again. I finally tell her, after all these years, it was not the goat. I have proven I can live with this hobble. Witnesses I cannot visit come to me. A longstanding record of favorable judgments has followed me and these figure to a formidable competence, which I demand she trust. But she nevertheless mocks that I must assist my leg with my arms.

"Grown men are free to walk and only worry their sashes as they mull."

She disturbs me. *Name to me a way in which I have been rendered less than a man!* If I respond loudly, Auntie will come and rapidly defend me, but I myself am in the trade of defense and will not fortify a retort with such force as to intimidate my own mother. I contemplate too long. She leans closer and kisses my forehead.

This tosses me backward.

> *I am six again. I took the greatest of care to not awaken my household but, once outside, steadily shuffled through the sands to the stable where the child lay. The backs of three daunting men did block the entrance, so I—short and slight—did duck underneath the roof at the side, how a bird may have, in pursuit of batting for her nestlings. A*

man's arm encircled the infant's mother's waist. I asked, only to be polite, was he the father? He said no. Her eyes were furtive. The child entranced me, and I stooped beside his trough. I had heard him cry; this was why I came. I knew nothing.

I knew much. I knew I must kiss him above his brow. He did not startle at this, my gift. A smear of the myrrh oil, which someone had applied to his head, left imprints of my dry lips.

My foot was now struck to a great depth, enflaming my entire right leg. The furious man at the back of the stable had done this to me and swung, again, the course of such luminescence its links must have been formed of true gold.

"Caspar! Your Majesty!" the man at the mother's side did intervene.

This man Caspar, then, must have been the child's father. Dark he was, beturbined, bold of build; whispering some chatter of consonants. Was he angry? Fearful? I could not read. The heavy smoke of frankincense choked me and did curtain each form and face from my gaze. I was becoming convinced that my ankle would stab me forever, so I would leave now and beg Mother's healing skill, though I so wanted to ask why no one had brought breads and cheeses or a bleating sheep, or even a woolen of sufficient warmth for the desert dark. What would an infant boy of Beit Lekhem ever do with fragrances and gold? Were these men mean or

*merely thoughtless? It would have been mine to ask.
I, after all, was a boy of this village.*

*But with terrible difficulty I slithered beneath the
low roof and made my escape. I would tell Mother
the goat did kick.*

With Mother long gone now, so many turns of seasons, Auntie feels constrained to make at least an occasional attempt to shepherd me, notwithstanding my gray locks and hoary beard. This evening, full of jabber, she wishes to know whether I have heard much of that child through the years. "He speaks of conciliation, forgiveness."

"Spoke," I say low. "He no longer walks among the living. And his scribes who are spoken of never themselves knew him."

"But *you* must have known he was special. You sneaked away to kiss him."

"Oh, my precious Sister of Mother, was it never plain? When I kissed him, I knew *I* was special."

In pivot, she partly veils a sanguine countenance I never was able to see upon my mother. I am sad for what cannot be, but I am circling Auntie like a ball on a string. *She is laughing.*

"Wait." I pour for us each a modest chalice of her wine. Her eyes invite this. She looks like she knows that I want us to go outside to dance in the dimming orange of sunset; that we shall be the shameless lame, flaunting to the heavens our trust in one another, seizing a moment of unmitigated joy.

Kellogg

I was used to this kind of thing. They don't call. Strangers like to confront me face to face. The three uninvited visitors who clomped up my front steps made soft taps on the door, probably to act sorry for their clatter. I do open to anyone who isn't armed with leaflets or a Bible, but I have this one quirk—I step outside so they can't help themselves to a glance at any of the research piles that lie wherever I was last reading through them.

"Michael von Grossenschwandt?" The diminutive one put the V in the W.

"Ausgezeichnet." I covered my heart like he had just won mine. "This is backwards though, fellas. We start with who you are."

They took on the contortions of three great blue herons pecking at bugs under their wings—synchronized business card fetching. Nicely done and, more important, obedient.

I like strangers to be obedient. So I waved them to the glider and my fake rattans. Okay. I had a VP and two executive directors, all from Husbandry Life and Casualty. The short one was sprouting beads of sweat. This was Omaha's early August, so I said I'd bring out some lemonade, but that triggered choreographic backhands all the way around. These guys could do theater. Just as well, this meant we were going to get right to it.

The heavier of the two big men spoke. "Your article has done considerable harm to our clients."

"Your *company*," I shot back, "has done considerable harm to them." My phone chimed a text in. "One moment, please."

From my father? A messageless jpg image for me to open whenever.

These guys were not visiting to complain about my article. They would try to talk me out of writing the follow-on I had hinted at in the wrap. If they had anything to discuss with me, they'd have argued fact. Their company is mutual, so their budget overruns and lost revenues do pass to their insureds as increases in premiums; obviously that was what their harm remark was about.

Tsk aw. I popped to my feet. "Well look, it's only ten. You head straight back to the office." I wagged a finger. "No stopping off for a quick nine."

They were once again obedient. Now in single file. I could tell the first one down the steps was their honcho. He was like a man moving along who'd just whistled for his two dogs to follow. This little regiment with its hierarchy—if one of them saw an opening, he could attack me from the flank—bristled me as much as the audacity of their attempt at shaming. It made me want to have a little fun with them. So I said without thinking, "You know, if I were to get a call from one of your investigators? A gesture to donate time doing research for my next article, which of course *would not* be about Husbandry, I'd have to give that some consideration, wouldn't I?"

I got to wondering, what did it cost Husbandry, this little visit? Three exec-salary hours. And what would the damage-control marketing set them back to publicly rebut my revelations? That's all these types care about, cost and ROI. Whatever their tally, it had to be smaller than the loss they figured to incur if I were, in fact, to write the follow-on.

I trailed them to the car to bid a special farewell. "Drive careful. You never know how funded your policy really is." Felt like I needed a shower from having been in their midst. I concede my self-righteousness can be ugly, but have you checked out evil lately?

Back on the porch, I punched up my phone to Outdoor Mode and was able to see the graphic from Dad pretty well. It was an exploded-view illustration of a longitudinal tibial plateau fracture, with a metal plate that reminded me of the sweep wings in the bottom of my grill, and with a half dozen screws for attaching the plate to the bone.

There are a lot of things I can't do. One is ever call my dad back right away. Let's see, forty years ago I was born, and he was in Montana. Mom sent word to him. What did he say when he got that news? *That's nice*, she told me, one day of my youth, when she felt like venting. He said, *That's nice*.

He was working the rails. This was before he became an engineer, but he couldn't just up and come home to Omaha because apparently the boss didn't look upon childbirth as a valid reason for time off, and you can't play loose with your RRB pension, now can you? So imagine holidays. Think of the Christmas his packages did arrive on time. For me there was a double gift: a model locomotive and an envelope with a note that said *Go see Malcolm*, a hostler at the Omaha roundhouse who would show me yard goats, push cars and pick freight. Which I might have done, had Dad troubled himself to jot my name on the envelope or even on a makeshift tag strung to the unwrapped locomotive. *Have fun in Whitefish, Dad*, I remember thinking. *Don't you worry about a thing back here.*

I guess it was a life. Once or twice a year we'd see him. Sometimes he'd send a stack of pictures.

"More personal than postcards," Mom pointed out. "You've got to give him credit for that."

We never punished him. Mom taught me not to. We only vowed not to become like him.

"You'd like it here in Kellogg, Mickey. We got three streets that cross the river, and every last Saturday, they close the bridge on one. We bring lawn chairs, and it's a town dinner right there above the river, only twelve bucks. Till the snows."

"I'm calculating, Dad. It's been three years since Mom died in Spokane and you moved yourself to Idaho. So you've been to…fifteen, twenty of these town dinners. You must have lots of friends by now. Can any of them take care of you for a while?"

"Oh, they're nice. But they all got things to do." To him this conversation was like playing a hole in golf. The town dinners bit was the wedge shot to drop the ball close, and this *they're nice-but-busy* line was his short putt. He's penciling his birdie in right now, chuckling.

Kellogg

It had taken him seven minutes to get around to telling me what kind of help he needed from me. I had cheated, of course, because that's what I do for a living—before he called me, I looked up how long a person with that break needs before they can bear weight on the leg. But now he wasn't being truthful about how long he wanted me to stay. He kept saying, *Two weeks, tops.* It's six.

I was doing my best anyway. "Well, tell me about these friends who are so nice but they can't help you."

"There's Sandra. She's out my front door," he said, "then her house is on the right." This is good. A writer like me appreciates this, telling it like you're putting him there. "She brings food sometimes, little tastes of whatever she made for herself. And there's Merrilee. She brought a plant today, says it'll grow fine in the dark house." And where does she live? "You look to the left." Good. He's bracketed by neighbors who don't hate him yet. But that's it now? Just two? "Well, there's Lloyd Ablitt, of course, with Merrilee." And what is he like? "Loyal, I guess you'd say." He'd steal a locomotive if you asked him to? "Not like that."

Loyal Lloyd with Merrilee in Kellogg. "Loyal and nice, or only loyal?"

"I just wouldn't mention Raini while you're here."

"I'm going to tell him the race of my ex-wife?"

"Just don't."

Bedroll, laptop and charger, t-shirts, underwear, socks, jeans, a few flannels, phone charger! Pills! Books, stickies, grill, tongs and flippers, spices, baggies, toiletries, flashlight, sneakers, shades, laundry bag. *Intelligence Report* from the SPLC. Yes, and a picture of Raini if I can find one. I hope.

My legs are numb from the twenty hours shaped like a car seat. And there were four hours of napping outside the truck stop in Rapid City, plus the time it took to calm down in Missoula, to walk the shoulder after I had pulled off 90 for a sandwich. Some jerk had closed back in too soon after passing me. I hit the gravel, and the Weber in the back fell over. I hope the guy has Husbandry for auto.

But I feel a calm over finally treading the floors of the house in Kellogg. I've already brought Dad's bed down to the living room. Well, gravity and I did. Lucky his bathroom is on the first floor here. Lucky he's got one of those Pat Boone tubs in there. Lucky I was indeed able to do my impression of an ant, making it up the narrow staircase with the couch on my back.

Fetch the mail. And start his car. I have no idea how long it's been since he drove it.

I'm behind the wheel idling, wasting a few minutes, deciding which ninety percent of the coupons I'm going to shitcan. A shadow falls across the burger place flier on the dash. I stab the window button down. He's peering at the top envelope in my hand.

So I push it to about ten inches from his eyeballs. "What do *you* think, mister?" I ask him. "Looks suspicious to me."

"What kind of a name is that, I was always wondering?"

"The sender?"

"No. The who it's to. Your daddy."

"Oh. Luka."

"No, the other one. The last one."

"They call that a surname."

"You don't wanna tell me? What kind of a name?"

I look over each shoulder, do my best fake scared, whisper, "A long name."

"I mean it now." He's huffing a little. "What kind of a name is it?"

I motion him close, then make him bend even closer. "Don't tell anyone? Please, it's a secret. It's jh…German."

The hulking brows on this impish old character are in spasm, confessing to me I've seeded a neurologic storm.

Well, then here comes lightning, just my way of saying bye. "Watch out walking home. Never know what nationalities are hiding in those bushes."

I guess I've met Lloyd.

I found a bottle of oaked chardonnay, couldn't believe they stocked it at the tight-quartered package shop on Cameron Avenue here. This is to bed down with, for that sleep I so badly need in order to both make up for all I've missed since Omaha and ready myself for bringing Dad home in the morning. For his mood, whatever that will be. I've already acquiesced to play the day according to his stream of consciousness. If the man wants to talk, I'll tune in or out at will. I'm sure he'll want to sleep, and the meds we get for him will help with that. I could use a doggy downer myself right now. But there is the wine.

I love labels. Moderately bold tang of ripened pear and fresh pineapple, with notes of aged oak and a smooth finish toward vanilla. My taste buds are sending a distress beacon, though. They're experiencing competition from a heavy, dark, offensive smell here in Dad's bedroom. It's everywhere, it's on everything. The scent of old man. Gears of Ferris wheel combine with rich undertones of electric razor debris and a hint of summer shirt collar in complicated dissonance with leather belt dry rot.

Since his bedroom is not going to work for me, I was already visiting options while the revulsion was peaking. I could sleep in the Expedition—let Lloyd wake me—or drag the couch cushions across the hall to Dad's tiny dump-and-run room, or see whether the sweet Google lady can find a store that sells nose plugs. I don't even know what nose plugs are. A paint store? It could be God doesn't even make nose plugs. Oh, sporting goods? For swimmers?

The junk room is sounding pretty good.

The rising sun had an unobstructed path to my pillow since there had never been a need to curtain the window in my repurposed bedroom. I can reconstruct how this space evolved from nothing at all to memorabilia to storage and staging. But I'm drawn to the rail route poster first. It's consistent with my recollections from postcards and postmarks. It's all there. Whitefish to Libby to Troy in Montana, to Bonners Ferry to Sandpoint in Idaho, on to Spokane without glancing Coeur d'Alene. The BNSF called this route the Kootenai River Line. I never knew that. And there's a color photo, pretty small, of five guys hanging off the ass end of a caboose. Dad thought enough of it to frame it. I'm examining his face, trying to appreciate the youthfulness in it, when my focus slides to the side and lands upon another of the caboose creatures—this one dark mustachioed and, more and more with assistance from my imagination and snoopy nature, resembling Lloyd. Is it? Let's say it is. Did one of them follow the other to Kellogg?

Lloyd must have been here first. So if Dad came later to buy the place next door, why had Lloyd had such a strong pull? Did one of them owe the other for something? Some extraordinary act that lifted the other's impending fate? And what type of reciprocation are they expecting or hoping for? Maybe this will jump out on its own. Or maybe I'll extract it from my dad like an inflamed tooth that must come out. Not soon, but certainly while I'm here.

The doctor had told me last night the surgery had gone well and not to try visiting "Mister Luke" until morning, but really, if I didn't show up until one in the afternoon to "collect" him, that would be best. So that gave me time to do the wash from his hamper, copy his friends' numbers from the fridge stickies into my phone, take fridge/freezer inventory and shop to restock, buy a longer coax that'll allow me to move the TV closer to his bed. I even picked up a long, flat pillow that should be great under his brace. We'll see. Cut the leg off a pair of his PJs. Found a sheet of five-quarter plywood, ripped it with ease on Dad's antique Delta table saw, to span from the Expedition passenger door to the front landing. Practiced with it. This will be handy for getting him to his follow-ups too. And it will blind him to the bottom step, the one he missed on his way down to the sidewalk, on his way down to breaking his tibia. We're going to think about recovery, not about why we have to recover.

The hard part of this morning was writing out rules longhand. No printer here, but I knew I'd have to lay down the law. So I used his short trip home to explain what the whip cracking was going to be about. "It'll be authoritarian. You can call me Benito."

He got misty on me, like he's so lucky to have me boss him around. We're going to get him off these drugs as soon as we can.

But when he told me Lloyd was coming over in a couple hours, and I said call Lloyd back and tell him tomorrow, not today, Dad fussed. I said, "Do it." He did. Then he bitched, good and feisty. All right.

Dad's been home a shade over 24 hours and hasn't been a problem for me in any way. He has eaten my cooking and said he enjoyed it. And he's strong like me, so he didn't have trouble keeping his right foot off the floor and supporting himself on the walker. He is getting restless, though. Over the water splashing on our lunch dishes, I can hear him in there trying to smooth something out; his sheets, maybe.

"Mickey, Lloyd is coming at three, in about ten minutes. Merrilee too."

"Good." I run upstairs to get a couple things and return. On the kitchen counter I open the *Intelligence Report* to the map that shows the hate groups in Idaho. On top of that I place the wallet photo of my black ex-wife. I tune the TV to the station that runs a pastoral landscape with nature sounds, and take two of the dinette chairs from the kitchen into the living room.

Merrilee is cheerful and soft-spoken, like getting hit with a marshmallow when you thought you were going to get hit with an apple. I resolve to stop wondering how she could have decided to spend her life with Lloyd, so this will help me as I try to act like Lloyd is welcome. The three are barely taking turns. They each can't wait to tell the next thing. Honestly, they sound like normal people.

It's hard to seize a slot in which I can interrupt, but with patience I do. "Lloyd, I'm going to pour some lemonades. Why don't you give me a hand." I lead him to the kitchen, where I've already got four tumblers sitting next to the hate map. "Merrilee is so sweet. You're lucky. Wish I was that lucky, but my marriage just didn't last. This is my ex-wife." I point. "Raini."

He shakes his head, but I can't be sure whether that's in pity of me or disapproval of her. "Was she out gallivantin' around?"

"No. I was." I lied, but so what.

Afterward, Dad thanked me for bringing out the lemonade. I told him, you don't thank people for lemonade, you just drink it till it's gone, then you get more. And if you can't buy more, you steal it. That it's one of the major food groups, way more necessary than water.

Everything had gone just as I had wanted it to. And now that everyone knows the rules, I can relax a bit.

Whenever Dad's physical therapist arrives, I feel no shame in bugging out. It's my big chance to get out of the house. There may be some nuggets of advice she conveys to him, but if there's anything I ought to be made aware of, he'll tell me. I always have things to do, useful things.

One is to keep going back to drug stores to get more syringes. These he uses for injecting heparin into his abdomen twice a day at eight o'clock. He has needed twenty, but no pharmacies around here could fill more than seven, four, five, and four because the stuff has a very short shelf life and it's expensive as hell, so they don't stock more than they figure they can dispense. I found this out only because there's one lonely, bored pharmacist who doesn't mind spilling the secret. All the others dispatched me with a partial, and a cheery *Come back and see us again*. Yeah.

Or I cut the grass, which gives me peculiar satisfaction until I always sink a heel into that soft area behind the tool shed where Dad turned the soil and then covered it with clippings. Today I've barely started the mower and I'm catching Sandra heading toward me. I've seen her once before and waved, but we've never met. She's gone a lot. She certainly wants to thank me for cutting her lawn when I'm cutting Dad's. It's so easy, though. These are postage stamp lots.

We introduce ourselves and she does thank me. She's an old hippie, I'm certain. She speaks well, and her straight gray hair runs to below her shoulders. I can picture her in bell bottoms. She very much appreciates that I've been mowing her lot, she says, because Hector has, without word, stopped coming by to do it. I know who she's talking about. He snowplows my dad's sidewalks in season. She hasn't seen Hector or his dog Blue for four or five weeks.

"He always brings Blue. Now Blue is a beautiful mix, part Australian, with that shiny bluish-silverish hair. You just don't see those around here. And he's missing an eye."

"I'll keep…looking for him in town." I almost said I'll keep an eye out for him. "Which eye?"

She points to her right eye. Smart. So there's no confusion. I wouldn't want to throw anyone else's heeler into the

Expedition someday. I pull out my phone on the spot and call Hector's number. I had copied it from the business card on Dad's fridge. Hector Manuelo Pacheco.

"No further information is available…" I've done such a faithful imitation of that halting artificial voice that I grin to give her permission to laugh.

But she's quite troubled. "Oh, dear," she says. "That man was the finest."

"I can try to find someone who'll work for you."

"No, no. I just will miss him terribly."

Hector, where did you go?

The lawns beckon. I'm pushing faster than I like. I think that's because I'm especially pleased to have been told I'm needed. But sure as shit, I've just rolled my ankle on that soft area, and I let go of the dead-man lever, and the motor shuts down. That's enough of that. So I march inside.

"So what's the deal with that patch you turned over, behind the tool shed? Did you plant yet?"

Dad says, "What patch?"

I'm out the back, getting the spring rake and a tarp and the spade. I feel a presence and spot Lloyd on his back porch. As soon as he sees me striding alongside the shed, he darts down the stairs and straight to me. *Blow it out your ass, Lloyd.* I'm pulling the clippings onto the tarp, which takes practically no time. I grab the spade.

"I wouldn't do that." He takes his hands off his hips as if he's going to try to stop me.

"Love to chat, Lloyd, but there's work to do."

"I mean it's all set. For your daddy to plant the garlics."

The plot is about six by three feet. Quick math tells me you can get about thirty cloves in the ground here, so his story has feasibility. But first let's do a little trust exercise.

"Dad changed his mind after he turned this over. Now he wants a paper birch, so I have to dig deep."

"Let's us go on in there," he says, and puts his palm out like an usher at a wedding.

I'd rather stay out here and start digging just to bother Lloyd, but my curiosity has me dropping the spade and leading the guy through Dad's back door. *How's Lloyd going to handle this?* But Dad's snoring, and I won't let anyone wake him. Ever.

"Okay, go away, Lloyd. I'm gonna to finish cutting." I drag the tarp to the back wall of the shed and put the rake and spade away, start the mower. He's glaring at me from his porch. *Fine. Glare all night.*

I mostly forgot about the patch through the following week. One morning early, I took a Nebraska call from an investigator named Shanice offering to do some pro bono research for me. I declined but I felt sorry for her since she'd surely been assigned to do this. She sounded both competent and confident. I asked whether she was contracted to Husbandry. She said no, she's an employee of theirs.

There were a few things. "See what you can find on a Lloyd Ablitt—A-B-L-I-T-T, male, currently in Kellogg, Idaho. Do not make contact or get close in your contacts. Get historical stuff. Particularly any involvement in hate groups, rallies. Debt and credit. Also, separately, Hector Manuelo Pacheco—P-A-C-H-E-C-O—possibly in Kellogg, possibly elsewhere in Idaho, in Washington or Montana.

Dropped out of sight five to six weeks ago. Handyman, landscape, snow removal. You may make contact. In fact, do. Tell him Luke's son is concerned. Also, Hector's dog has not been seen, name Blue, part blue heeler, aka Australian cattle dog, male, missing his right eye. Last known to have been with Hector in Kellogg. I'm saying, see if you can find Blue as well."

She asked how soon I needed this.

I said sixteen days or fewer would be best. I wanted it while I'd still be in Idaho. "And Shanice, thank you. Track your hours to the tenths if you would. Track your costs; I don't mind reimbursing those. Nothing is off the books with respect to my tax liability. Anything to report, call me. Any questions, text me. If I have any news for you, how do you prefer to get it?"

Shanice is sharp. Who'd have thought anything would come of my encounter with Moe, Larry, and Curly?

I ran downstairs to fix breakfast. I asked Dad to call Lloyd, see whether he could come over, fix lunch, help him in and out of the tub, stay with him till around three. I told him I needed a break and I wanted to check out Coeur d'Alene. "Personal time. And while I'm gone, maybe Lloyd's visit will refresh your memory, and you can answer that question I asked you a week ago. Who owes who. The truth would be good."

I got the dishes put away, slid the laptop into its bag, and I was gone.

The lakeside table is fantastic, and the sky and the water are fighting over which is the deeper azure. When I can ignore the yachtsmen performing swagger for their impressionable guests in their impressive bikinis, I'm in such a mellow place. Glass of wine. Add sunshine. I have my folio out, as if being prepared to note some thoughts will lead to having any.

Shanice calls. She found Hector already, spoke to him. He's in temporary convalescence at a nursing home in Silverton. He fell off a roof, "but get this: Blue bolted when no one responded to his barking. He went looking for help. He found a man all the way across town who was willing to follow, and Blue led the guy to the house where Hector fell, but the paramedics had already hauled Hector to Kootenai hospital in Coeur d'Alene. Of course, this guy had no way of knowing about that, so he took Blue into his own home. But after about a week, the guy's wife pitched a fit and he had to take Blue to the pet rescue by you in Kellogg, where the staff remember getting a call the previous week from a nurse asking about such a dog, but nobody had made a record of who it was that called. So even if Hector had somebody try, they've given up by now."

She tells me Hector could be discharged to go home as soon as two weeks from now. "You can't call him on his cell—that phone broke in his fall." I thank Shanice profusely. She says she has tentacles out on "that other subject" but expects it will take a while for answers to stream in.

I call the shelter, say I'm in CDA but on my way back to Kellogg, where I will be paying Blue's get-out-of-jail fees and caring for him until Hector can. They say they've never done this before—release an animal to someone other than the owner they've identified. I say, well, I've never done this before either—stood in for a disabled pet owner. "Gosh, do you think we can help each other get through this? Improvise a little? Or crawl in a hole. And by the way, write down exactly what kind of food he needs and how much, unless that's something else you never do."

Really, the lady at the shelter was trying her best to be nice. She deserved better.

I call the nursing home, introduce myself to Hector, tell him my plan for Blue. Sandra was right. Apparently I can go straight to Heaven now. Hector says so, and he *is* the finest man. Better yet, he's not missing. Best of all, he's not buried behind my father's shed.

Dad is agitated about my plan to bring Blue to his house. He even says we don't know anything about "that dog," despite that he has petted Blue several times.

I tell him, "Look, I'll take care of both of you. I have two people to take care of, one gray, one blue. What's the big deal?"

"I never had a dog."

"You never had a family either." I know that's low, but I can go lower. "If you prefer, I'll pack up and stay with Blue at Hector's apartment. Just say the word."

Dad puffs. "Find out if he bites."

"Don't worry, I'll tell him *you* do."

I think of my dad's first mention of the dinners on this bridge. I instantly pictured soup overtopping a bowl because of the slope. It has me grinning now, and two folks nearby notice. The bridge is so flat that a ball would have trouble rolling. Below us is a stream, a river in name only for the volume it will collect as it continues westward. The couple ask me what's so funny, and I tell them, and they don't laugh with me. But they like my dopey little plastic tray with folding legs, think it's "so practical."

Ah, great. The aluminum raking the pavement is Lloyd's lawn chair, and he has invited himself to join me. I had seen him sitting alone back near the buffet tables, Merrilee not with him.

"I've been thinking about that name of yours."

I'll bet he has. "All right, Lloyd, I'll unlock the mystery for you. It means from the wide valley. So then yours would be von Kleinenschwandt, from the narrow valley. Feel better?"

"There's something I want to show you."

I tell him that's nice but I've got to get this brisket home to my dad. I promised. First I'm getting a brew from the keg, does he want one? He nods, and that surprises me.

I sit sipping, admiring the hues of the saturating dusk, wishing it would slow a bit, feeling I'm not done with this day yet. I'm aware Lloyd's been studying me, but I must congratulate myself for not having let him distract me. I would like to say shut up and drink your beer.

"This thing I want to show you, you might want to write about it in your book. Luke told me you're a writer. You make up stories."

"I don't need a reason. I'll walk with you, as long as it's not far out of our way."

"Four, five blocks. Six."

We're headed northeast, away from the river, and it's still residential. I'm drawing some comfort from that. It would have been eerie following the crackpot into the woods or a warehouse. We are close to the outer edge, though. We can almost touch the rising forest, in the Italian Gulch area, as best I can tell. On this lot we're coming to, instead of a house, a shed sits, larger than a park-your-tractor but smaller than what you'd call an outbuilding. We followed a tight path that twice hooked around overgrowth taller than me.

Lloyd has used his phone to disarm the security system, which doesn't chirp or flash in confirmation, looked like it just changed a red dot to green. He uses a key to open a bolt near the top of the door and another for the bolt near the bottom. And now he has to roll a combination into the Master to free up the latch. So for this final act, he orders me to turn away, and for the second time tonight I can't wipe a stupid grin off my face. I set the folded tray and chair and the dinner box on the grass. He pulls me into the shed and closes the door. Only then does he flip on the lights.

Before me is nothing but the chipboard floor hosting so many semiautomatic weapons you couldn't walk through. You would have to kick them aside. In one corner is a pile of pistols, in another what appear to be disproportionately deep stacks of magazines and ammo boxes. The math I run tells me these things, in sum, are of much greater value than his home.

"You suck as a housekeeper," I tell him. "Ever heard of shelves?"

"That's it, then," he says. He flips the switch. Black goes the shed, and he guides me out.

We half see, half feel, the walk home. Light is only intermittently available from certain porches of the little homes. They don't bother with sidewalks here, but thank goodness the paving is pretty smooth. I'd hate to stumble and drop the styrofoam takeout box. I truly did promise I'd bring Dad the brisket, but also I'm enjoying its squeaks—the carton sends an annoying rasp into the air and makes it feel acceptable I don't chat the whole distance with Lloyd. But I know I'm going to be the one breaking the silence.

"All right. What does Merrilee think of your blowing all that family money on guns?" We're almost back to his place, and I'm not done with him after all.

"Them ain't mine. They're my son's." He had told me his son lives in Priest River, and that's going on two hours away.

"That's quite a drive for him to have to make every time he wants to off a Jew or a nonwhite. Or an occasional infant, because you know what those grow up to be. The fella must be so dedicated."

"Are you gonna write about this in your book?"

I go with the first crap that comes to me, about the creative process and how complicated it is, "because complicated is what sells books, isn't it?"

"This is important, Mickey." It's almost a whine. "You should write about it. How worried a dad can be for his son. How much it hurts. I could buy him a copy."

I say Good night, Lloyd—that way, with his name—and turn to Dad's house, but I pick up Lloyd's footfalls behind me.

His whisper whooshes over my shoulder, strained and hot. "Same as your own daddy loves you."

"You told Lloyd I'm writing a book." I'm ambushing Dad and I know that's not fair, given he can't stand up and walk away. And he's trying to have his morning cereal in peace. "What'd you do that for?"

"I wasn't going to tell him you're a journalist. The man's paranoid as it is."

"I'm a journalist, not a leper. But he thinks I'm writing a novel and—what do you know—he isn't uneasy about that at all."

"Grab the milk?"

"I've still got a few more weeks in this town, Dad. Plenty of time for you to remember any other lies you've spread, in case you'd like to let me in on those."

I have to have privacy for my next move. I'll do the short drive up to Silver Mountain, set up at one of their outdoor tables by the base of the gondola. Make the call.

I keep trying to slow my thoughts so I won't sound like this is an emergency. They won't slow. "Please look into Ablitt's son in and around Priest River. Do not make contact. Get comings and goings, definitely up to Sandpoint and even as far as Bonners Ferry. Sources of income, arrests. Any licenses, permits. Email it all as a single PDF. In a week and a half? And before the weekend. The print shop is closed Saturdays and Sundays. So for those days, my alternative is an 80-minute round trip."

She asks, "Weapons?" Shanice is amazing.

"Dropping out of his nose."

It's strikingly beautiful, the nursing home in Silverton. Getting Hector into the Expedition wasn't as hard as I thought it would be. In fact, he's been having PT and OT here, and I've already concluded he'll be able to take care of himself after I stock his cupboards and fridge. He's hugely grateful to me but beyond disappointed I didn't bring Blue. And I'm going to take in the groceries and set him up with his new burner phone before I pick up Blue to run him to Hector's. I'm sure I'm no longer qualified for immediate entry to Heaven.

The reunion overwhelmed me. All I did was set Blue's kibble canister on the counter, pointed to it, suggested to Hector "Four, four thirty," and left.

I'm getting into my car, and who do I notice is strolling toward Hector's building? It's my good buddy Lloyd, toting a casserole without Merrilee in my field of vision. One of us is nuts. I just always thought it was him.

I've got the Expedition ready to set sail for Omaha. The last week has been as busy as any since I've been in Idaho. I put the garlic cloves into the ground with extreme care to trap the blunt side, root side, down. I had Sandra, Merrilee and Lloyd, and Hector and Blue over to Dad's for baby backs I smoked on the Weber. It was the first time I heard steady laughter and saw what joy looked like, first time in what feels like forever. I hauled Dad's bed up the stairs and brought the couch back down, and made him strut through his house with the walker, but using both feet. And practice the stairs up and down.

There's a fistful of banded cash next to the coffee maker. This means Dad asked Lloyd to go to the bank for him. For me. Of course there's no note, not even a sticky with my name on it. But there is a four-by-six shot of me at bat in my Little League uni.

I hold it up. "Tired of keeping this?" That sounded a bit sarcastic, but I'm not in a mood to apologize.

"That's a copy I asked Lloyd to get printed for you. I'll never part with the one your mom sent, with the message on the back. It saved my life."

I have no idea what he's referring to. "And you couldn't save hers."

"I did, Son. I did. Just not the last time. Anyway, those things are between her and me, and those stories go in the ground, where they belong. You *can* ask about the good times, the tender bits, whenever you're ready. You're entitled to that."

"I got to go soon."

"I know."

My work here is done, except for one thing. One daunting thing. We sit over our coffees at the dinette. I've come back inside with the two identical manila envelopes, one of which I remove the stack of papers from.

"Dad, I have something grave to reveal to you. I'm sure you've been unaware of it. I have a responsibility to take this to the authorities, and it would be unfair for me to leave without letting you know about this."

I slide the stack to him. He gapes, turning the pages. I tell him I saw the cache. I tell him I remember exactly where it is. I tell him innocent people could die. I tell him I'm so very sorry.

I tell him there's one thing that can stop me—he and Lloyd can discuss this, take it to the authorities themselves, and then have them confirm to me they did. "…which might hold you two together through the times ahead. If *I* were to do it, Lloyd might hate you, vicariously. Forever."

I know Dad'll say he won't have a thing to do with this. I know he'll think, or maybe even say, that I am a traitor and how could I? Who do I think I am? He's quiet and motionless. He rises and announces he has to pee.

When he returns, he stands behind me, his hands on my shoulders. "So brave you are."

"People could die, Dad."

"Yeah, and we must prevent that," he says.

"Children and many innocent people."

"It's already out of our hands. The only question was whether to go local, or state, or federal. We went federal. Mickey, I don't want you to ever regret getting involved." Dad produces a business card to enter into my phone. It's from his ATF agent. It's tattered. It's been places.

"How the hell was Lloyd ever able to make *that* decision?"

"He needed me. I can't keep you posted, Mick. Been told to keep my mouth shut, but you can contact this guy yourself."

The hug beats any I've ever had with this man.

Near the 90 ramp I slanted into an empty gravel lot and stepped out. There's a pretty broad look at Kellogg from here. Its features and its mood feel proud. I made it quite a long look until this morning's chill asserted that this place is real. That this is no video. This is no snapshot. I am no tourist.

Clamped under my wiper blade had been a bon voyage note with a lazy and looping signature facing out.

from
Sandra

It's still in my jacket pocket, where I put it to read for encouragement whenever I might want some. It's kind of early to want some, but I do.

I wish you peace, it says. I was sure it would say *Wishing you a safe trip home*. But no, I wish you peace. She may as well have scribbled *Don't you turn 41 still hateful*. It was never out of compassion I attended so faithfully to Luke. That was plain as day. It was only to show the old man it's always within your ability to properly care for your family. This was my work here, the big thing that's finally done. That's what everyone, including I guess Sandra, watched me do.

So now I wonder, can anyone ever do the job I asked Raini to do and then wouldn't let her—to block my bent toward vengeance and keep shoving me toward fairness? I suppose the voices of Kellogg will try to have their way with me on the long, long drive and I believe I'll let them.

Nosy SOB

Will was out for lunch, idling his new used Kia in the work lot and ruminating on the tensions that pervaded the model shop inside. Fewer engineers had been bringing their designs downstairs. Little work is uncomfortable. No work is death.

Management still considered the shop a profit center that loses money instead of a cost center that no one should expect to return profit. And Engineering could have easily afforded to take over the shop from Services—Will was certain of that—and fund it as a necessity of their own. But they didn't. Every one of the technicians could foresee what was coming to their otherwise proud careers.

So this February noon, Will was stepping out. Lunch at his bench would get him either an earful of today's twist on dread or a hush that would have his butt shifting on his stool.

He *was* hungry, but it wouldn't be like the old days, when he would make the stop-and-go jaunt to Benatti's for an Italian beef soaked in hot giardiniera, and at least three pints of Old Style. Just the freedom to do that seemed to always constitute a damn good excuse for a wet lunch. All he was driving out for today was a couple avocado rolls at Your Asia and a hot tea to sip. He was going to savor this hour, not race the clock like before.

But first, the cars. *All these cars.* He recalled the years when everyone assumed the northern Illinois tech boom had plateaued and traffic could get no worse. That was when the crisscrossing six-lanes with their interstate ramps already had retail driveways too close to those intersections. *...to accept the things I cannot change.* No need to finish the silent prayer. It was second nature.

Bernadette. This jam-up reminded Will of her, of the way she used to carp about this tangled mess. Bernadette—talented, cheerful, candid. *Don't forget tan.* Tall enough to speak with authority, though she had none, but soft enough to take it all back with a moment's apologetic pause. Her helmet of straight neck-length auburn curiously made her prominent in any gathering. At least Will thought so. The only woman of the seven technicians, all young but one. *Queen of the Internet.*

For so many months she'd been bugging Will to "get out there again and date." He considered this to have been getting into his space. You don't do that in tight work quarters. But then one day, she said she'd try to stop. "I'm giving up on you." And then she really did.

Ahead there was trouble. The six-lane was always knotted and dragging, but now it was stalled. Will figured to cut into the Home Depot service road, wend a bit, borrow Walmart's garden center driveway, and dump out into the alley behind the strip center where Your Asia leases its space. He made that cut and climbed.

But his "nosy SOB" mind, as Bernadette often called it, stole a look from the rearview. It was a two-car, a big Cadillac or something had T-boned the front quarter panel of a little thing, possibly a Prius.

Will saw himself as someone who's useful in any emergency but here, now, he was in jitters. He popped the back hatch and grabbed the wool blanket he'd bought for this rare purpose on his vacation last fall in Maine. *One useful thing.*

He slid on his soles down the slushy grade and banged first on the driver's window of the Cadillac. The old woman would not unlock the car. Would not or could not. Maybe she thought Will was the other driver and he was mad at her. Will came to realize he was the only person out on the pavement.

He needed to check the guy in the Prius. He tapped on the driver's window. This door was unlocked. A waft of air bag choked him into spastic coughs.

The guy wasn't a guy! She was a slender young woman in a tight wool plaid coat and a purl flap beanie that let waves of strawberry blond slither out.

"Are you okay? Are you? Are you okay?" He unfolded the blanket, laid it across her, resisted his inclination to tuck it under her shoulders. He noticed, with the engine dead, the heater was pushing chilly outside air through the industrial atmosphere of air bag. He shut it off. *One smart thing.* "Are you warm enough?"

Her lips were moving, but she wasn't producing anything audible.

"I'm sorry, try again?" Will's throat clenched. He wiped his nose on his glove. "Try again, sweetie."

She was able to whisper, "I like your coat," but now gave in to the will of her drooping eyelids. There would be no more looking, no more talking.

Will had to shut the door to preserve whatever heat the little car still held. He sprinted to the passenger side to slide in there and keep her company. It was locked. So he had to go back and unlock all the other doors, as he *should have done right away*.

But a firm slap on the shoulder from behind stopped him. "All right, buddy. Go back to your car. We're taking over." It was a paramedic, who had reinforcements and equipment trailing. "That is, if you weren't part of this or affected by it."

Will didn't say it. That he was affected.

The responsible soul he had been working so hard to become, Will phoned back to the office, told boss Darnell about the snarl and that he'd be late coming back from lunch.

"Do your best," Darnell said.

"What best?"

There were many things Will was resolved to not mention in the AA meetings, even though—as the Big Book coaches—he was one of the club's most helpful to others. He never felt he was failing to open up when he held back things that were bothering him. The Steps were there for him to sort stuff with, to be guided by. He relegated his irritants to the very rear of his consciousness, where they always expire or they shut the hell up. In fact, Will was quite good at this relegating.

All right, there *were* things to discuss, but he was a good listener to himself. He also knew that the offer from his Higher Power to do some of that listening, when he humbly accepted it, brings the serenity. So his frequent intervals of silent reverence continued without a need to grope for the right words to use.

One irritant, of course, was the frequent muttering of the management team about the shop's looming fate. In recent stop-bys, Darnell had been dropping comments like, "Have you guys seen what's happening to our 401(k)s?"

Oh, no, the smirks from Will and Bernadette and a couple of others answered back. *It's our fault we're underused. And how dare we drag down everyone else's retirement nest eggs? Can we please be terminated?* This was the uncomplicated of the two nags on his inner peace. There was also the cumbersome nag, this other one having been of his own invention.

These were supposed to be happy times. At fourteen months clean, he was no longer admonished by the Program to avoid the start of any relationship with a woman. The risk of relapse from potential heartbreak was no longer greater than the risk of relapse from loneliness. All the meetings, pizza and coffee, bowling and coffee outings with like-minded friends could now be interspersed with dates, even dates with a normie. But whenever Will dared to consider an acquaintance for a date, he was haunted by a recollection of the young woman from the accident. "I like your coat."

Were those the last words she ever spoke? Did she mean the coat he had on or did she think the blanket was his coat? Did she want him to lay his coat over the blanket? Or had she seen something in him—a kind spirit or his concern for her—something she thought would be good in her life?

Nosy SOB

In his first year of recovery, he'd had plenty of time to imagine what sort of pursuit he would one day make toward a romantic involvement. He had tended to hope for a slow start. One with an egress propped open behind him but also a genuine desire to amble forward, boldly into it.

The late-April storms were booming, humidity was making cameos, softball was beckoning. These burst into his days. In all previous years, he welcomed their return. But this year they represented alarms whose message he understood, that precious time was evaporating. And this is to be feared when something needs doing. Something he'd been *doing squat about*.

A text gonged in.

Had 2 ck w you. R u still at the shop

Bernadette had been let go in early February. "Too much time spent browsing on her phone," Darnell said.

His point was part logical. Part horseshit, though, because she often had been the conduit for how the other technicians got their toughest work questions answered. Will quickly typed her back, lots had been happening there, maybe they'd best catch up. So she invited him to her complex's clubhouse for a Saturday afternoon non-party party. He'd bring a thermos, he figured.

"So…are you seeing anyone?"

Will wasn't surprised she asked, just a little surprised that a good half hour had passed before she did. "Did you ever try to find anybody?" he asked her. "Public records, that kind of thing? But where you don't even know their name."

"First off, you whimsical SOB, you don't just go and decide you want to strike something up with somebody you don't even know the name of."

Will told his story.

"Come." Bernadette set her half-full Solo cup on the newel and dragged him by his arm, through the gate and all the way to her condo.

Her keyboard was already chattering by the time he pulled up the extra chair. "We need a credit card. I'll fill out this stupid PDF for you...Oh, whoa. We can't do anything. 'Cause we don't know her license plate number."

"But I do."

"No. Serious?"

"When the paramedic shooed me, I read the plate."

"You nosy SOB. Did you write it down?"

"It wrote itself down in my brain."

"Crazy, crazy SOB."

Will slapped his credit card on her desk. Bernadette slapped her thigh, and there went her fingers again. A nervous mouse behind a wall is what the sound reminded Will of, but it felt sort of reassuring.

Not so satisfying, though, when he thought about it, given they'd have to sit again after the response from the DMV would land in Will's inbox. *That could be a whole week.*

With the accident report in hand, and a name—Lauren McCollum—they visited online records, two of which they used Will's credit card again to pay for, and did "the Zaba thing." They concluded there was good reason to believe

Lauren still lived, and they even found a social media clue to where she probably worked, in a building not far from Will's campus. On the other side of the six-lane, which made sense, Bernadette said, "if you think about it. About the direction she was going when her car got hit." Bernadette had come through.

Someone at the AA club knew a guy who Will thought worked at the company Lauren appeared to work for, a guy who could look up her work number. This was good, because Will was way too much the gentleman to just show up at her office. So he thanked Bernadette profusely at the door.

She said, "You must have really seen something in that girl. Just be careful of your ass. Or I'll kick it."

He cackled and twisted the knob to let himself out. But she was quick enough to smack a wet kiss on Will's neck.

Darnell was the one from the club. *How to get the contact info without sucking up? Just* don't *suck up.*

But Darnell never disappoints when you expect him to be a prick. "And I should do this why?"

"So I can look for a job over there. You approve of that, don't you?"

Darnell huffed and read out the number from his phone.

Will thought that was too easy, so he called the guy as soon as he had shut Darnell's door. Get to him before Darnell had a chance to tank the request. Yes, Darnell was that reliably mean. Yes, Darnell needed some remedial step work. But none of that mattered once the guy over there answered his desk phone.

All Will had heard Lauren utter was the whisper. Today she sounded just as sweet as he had imagined. And she remembered him. She said, "I couldn't honestly tell you right now what color your hair was, but yeah."

"I feel like apologizing for not trying to contact you earlier, you know, to give you my best wishes for your recovery. I mean, you could've needed—"

"Oh, I didn't. Everything was fine. And I have good people all around me. They wouldn't have let me get down or anything like that, so don't fret, okay?"

"I thought it would be nice to see you. In person, even though, you know, there's…nothing to catch up on really, since…we didn't know each other before that."

Lauren let this sink in or finish whatever it was doing in her ear. "Well, tell you what. I still have your blanket. They wanted to throw it out, and I told them I'd be the patient from hell if they did. So see? I've been meaning to give it back all along."

"I really don't need it back. I just would enjoy seeing you."

"No, really, it's yours. Besides, we've been talking lately about making amends."

Is she in the Program? Think, damn it. Think. He was letting too much dead air pass, so he briskly set up a lunch for the next Tuesday. He would drive. He made one more call, then traced the hall back to Darnell's office to announce, "I'm leaving an hour early today. Got an interview."

The jerk just stared.

The coffee aroma was so heavy he felt like he was walking into a meeting. Bernadette dragged him in, the same way she had on that Saturday from the clubhouse. Will had said, when he called from the shop this afternoon, he just wanted to update her on The Lauren Situation—"No biggie." She pulled him to the couch, where a full mug sat steaming away right across from him. But she clutched both his hands and was not going to let go. Those white nails, the pearls tipping her tan fingers, they said so by their pinch.

"I'm in AA," Will told her.

"I know. So what?"

"You know? How do you know?"

"Well, first, Doofus, you stopped coming into the shop smelling like booze every morning. Also, the thermos to a clubhouse party? Come on. Anyway, I've got it on my last year's calendar, just when it was you became a new man. And plus, Darnell told me. Not right away, not when you joined up or whatever you call it. Around the turn of this year. Yeah, he said he'd hate to have to let you go. When things get worse for the shop? Something about brothers."

"That asshole."

Bernadette tightened her grip. "Why did you want to tell me this?"

Will recounted the conversation with Lauren from this afternoon, her use of the word. "Amends. I mean she could be in AA or NA. That's bad, if that's the case. Well, not the best. Or maybe it's something at church, if she goes to church. And she used the word We. I don't know who We is, but it's got to be people who decided *together* to clean up some things they've done. She could be married or living with somebody. I just don't know anything."

"Look at you, you're shaking. Listen to me, Will—what you wanted was to talk with her. You've done that and you'll do more on Tuesday. Meaning, you've got what you wanted. It's not that you wanted her, it's that you wanted to find out *about* her. Look…right now, this minute, would you say you want her? Shhh. No, you wouldn't. Because you might not even like her." Bernadette stood and lugged his hands all the way to the door. "Go. Go in peace. Go to a meeting, if that's what you do. But I'm telling you, Will, you're a mess when you're uncertain. Maybe we all are, but man, you're a pro."

"It's just—"

"Scary. Scary till Tuesday." Bernadette shook her head so gently. That auburn hair washed back and forth like curtains to a zephyr. Her mouth still a bit open made her more puzzled looking than he remembered ever seeing her. And she whispered, "If you want something else to think about in the meantime," then she pressed her lips to Will's. Dropped his hands, shoved him out of the condo. But she did hold her tug of the nip she'd grabbed of his shirt, up until the lethargic door had almost finished easing itself closed between them.

And now Will won't touch his cheek—where Bernadette's hair swished against it.

Master of Quiescence

My husband Carl is a man of few words until, in the rare moment, his words will burst into the atmosphere like a murmuration of starlings that assemble a fast-moving cloud and hijack everyone's attention. The first time we made love, the good man cried all over my face. Only after our breathing returned to near normal did I ask him why. He shook his head *No*.

But was it *Don't ask me that, Sally* or just *I'm not sure?* I trusted he would one day tell me, when he was ready to, but over the next two days, my imagination pitched various reasons at me; reasons that devolved from a lofty *I was thinking, why can't every moment of our lives be as beautiful as this* to *I'm afraid I can't be the man you're hoping right now I am*, all the way to *God, do I miss Sofi*.

Still I did not press him for the answer. Two days descended into nightmares of my own contrivance, until the phone rang.

"I have to have a buffalo steak," were his words. "I woke up thinking about this. How about Harvey's tonight?"

"Sure," I told him. "Are you having a good day?"

"Nnn, we can talk about that. The theme du jour in the office seems to be Forgetting. Everyone is forgetting what they promised. Forgetting what I said and when they're supposed to be where. Look, I'll make the reservations. Oh, and your answer is I never thought I would feel so loved. More on that later too, okay?"

"Sure," I said, and for the first time in our blossoming relationship, I didn't want either of us to say one word more.

I would realize years later that the busiest times of our life together were the happiest. This could have been because neither of us had the energy to waste allowing any disagreement to get protracted; or because we were always building something—house, family, or a dream for much later; or because, being busy, we were doing exactly the things we wanted to be doing, and why on earth wouldn't that keep you happy?

So the little people—Erin and, two years after that, Shane—came along, and I suppose there were some bumps but I don't remember any. This is what we'd wanted: two. Visions realized, hopes satisfied. A ribbon and bow were drawn around the package we had made. There would be more packages. We just didn't know what those might be.

That is how I expressed it to Carl. "I mean, you couldn't give me one thing more to make me any happier."

"Well, I'm sure glad you feel that way," he said, then took several half steps backward.

"Carl?"

"I'm gonna...go look at the garage door opener; it's making too much noise, the chain."

"Carl."

"What?"

I just shook my head, and he slipped through the kitchen and mud room on quieter than his real feet until the door to the garage sucked shut like a refrigerator.

An old darkness spread across me, unwelcome but undeniable. It wasn't pessimism—I wasn't waiting for a shoe to drop, I was just gravely uncertain.

When I started thinking food may never taste right again, I called my mother. She was always the opposite of Carl, she would talk to me. Within a minute-and-a-half, she asked whether he could be longing for something. I told her—I even was a little short when I did—that my whole point was we had everything we had longed for. That's when she asked me, had he been longing for something before we'd met?

The next morning I took the kids to the shallows in the high end of the river canyon after Carl went to work. There is a hollow in the stone right above the narrow section where they loved to play. I nestled into it, like so many times before, to let my thoughts wander wherever they wished. I recalled how he had held me so hard his arms shook the night he cried in my face. His explanation from two days later came back to me. Then I remembered my suspicions from before he explained. I knew—I knew it then and I knew it now—he wasn't missing Sofi. But there in my little cave, my thoughts about his ex-girlfriend landed on what I might have been looking for. Okay, let's say he was not longing for Sofi, but he had told me how the whole thing with her had ended badly and that he expected to always feel *incomplete* about it. I climbed down and splashed some water on the kids, then hopped back into my nook to plan some repair work.

That night, after we put Erin and Shane to bed, I crossed in front of Carl on his way to the TV and said I had something to tell him. I told him I had been the ringleader of a bunch of A students in my high school as we made raucous fun of my chemistry teacher in the courtyard outside his office. A female teacher walked into his office while I was hooting about him. This I know because I heard his voice, loud and clear, louder than my own, when he said hello to her. "He never approached me about having mocked him, never even gave me a sneer, and he aced me for the class. Well, junior year in college, I wrote the man a letter to set things straight, saying I had done him wrong that day and that he had been a big influence on me as I continued my education. And that I would always be grateful for having had him as a teacher."

"That's a lovely story," Carl said, without a hint of sarcasm.

"Well, I remembered it today at the canyon, and now it occurred to me you might like hearing about it, especially in case there's someone…I don't know…you'd like to set something straight with."

"Like who?"

"Oh, I wouldn't know," I said, but understood that I would need to prod. "This is where *your* stories come in, isn't it?"

Carl crossed his arms, scratched his elbow. "I really am okay with my parents," he said. He bit his lip. A silent interval fell, and I couldn't tell whether he was feeling more awkward than I was. I realized that, if both of us felt awkward, then it didn't matter who felt more awkward.

He was going to give up, so I slapped my knees to stand, but then out came, "I ran a fastball in on the thigh of one kid in college, and that was deliberate. I hated the way he smirked at me when he stood on second base a couple innings earlier. But I'm not writing him a letter."

"Of course not." I picked up the remote and handed it to Carl. "Well, maybe there's someone. Didn't you once tell me things ended not so well with Sofi?"

"Ho!"

Strike up an orchestra.

"I sure did," he said.

The next evening he sat down to write. He already had two pages that I could see done, likely from some free time at work. I asked him, wouldn't he feel more comfortable at the desk in his office; the dining room table seemed too public a place. He said no, that he has never had anything to hide from me. My heart jumped. *Strike up a choir of angels* for this saint. He offered to read it to me when he finished, but I said the only thing that mattered was that he'd said in it everything he felt ought to have been said.

He nodded. He said the whole exercise was like broadcasting a radio program. If Sofi's radio picked it up, fine.

Months passed without a response from Sofi. Carl didn't acknowledge this to me, but he didn't have to. Having a saint in the house makes everyone remarkably intuitive.

Midway, after about the first whole month, he grabbed my hands one day as soon as he came in the door after work. "Yes," he said. "There is a ribbon and bow around the package you and I have made. And I am happier than I ever imagined I could be. It was the only truly great pitch I ever made, and you caught it. Now, I'm hungry. How 'bout Harvey's?"

The stream behind the shed froze solid before a response from Sofi arrived. I picked it out of the mailbox and put it, intact, on Carl's desk.

After the kids' off-to-bed time, he brought it, opened and crinkled, for me to read.

> Well Carl or should I say Snarl because that's the
> way you looked at me the last time I saw you. I
> must say you took me by surprise here. Things
> have changed like we knew they were going to so
> you didn't have to tell me this like it's some kind
> of news. I thought to enclose a picture of my
> husband and my son but I don't want to because I
> don't want you to write back and say how
> handsome they are or anything like that. The fact
> is when you left I lost almost twenty pounds and
> then when people were good to me I gained that
> all back plus another twenty, so I was fat and I
> didn't even recognize myself. There must be some
> good reason why people suffer like this and I guess
> religions think it's good but I don't, not so much.
> I will wish you that things go how you want them
> to go and that's about all I can say. Nice you
> thought about me but like I said when it was over,
> let's just both have our nice lives.
>
> Sofi

Halfway through, my palms stopped sweating, my attitude graduated from *Oh god, Sofi, don't make him want to communicate with you any further* to *Sofi, you bitch*, to finally *Carl, I feel so sorry for you.*

I was careless in telegraphing these thoughts with tears.

"No, don't," Carl said. "This has been a wonderful experience."

"Is somebody making lemonade? You're not calling her letter wonderful."

"Nope. There is nothing wonderful about her letter."

"Then what was?" I had to get this answered.

"The waiting. It can be energizing, can't it? To toss something out there and not know what'll come back? You know the feeling."

On the pillow, the same pillow his tears had soaked on that otherworldly night many years before, I slid to park my lips next to his ear.

"Carl…I have to tell you something. I never made fun of my chemistry teacher, so I never sent him a letter to apologize. Does that make you mad?"

"Nope."

"Is it all right with you that I made up that story?"

Carl made a big exhale. "Well, I wish you weren't telling me this. It was better before."

"Why? What was better?"

He puffed out a little chuckle. "The waiting. Waiting for you to tell me this."

I could sit tight, the way Shane and Erin anticipate Christmas, and eventually find out how he had been able to see through my ruse. So I let myself freefall, deep and deeper. I let the pillow accept this soul of mine. A curtain of my hair drew closed and it insulated me in the cube of white I just love, where I'm definitely not awake but I think I'm not quite asleep either. A man was standing at what must have been the front door, holding three cartons of eggs under each arm. He kept insisting he wasn't late. Finally he said, *You know I couldn't bring these to you till I saw what they were.* I turned away from the man to take the eggs to the kitchen, but in that moment, Carl rolled over and whispered to me.

"Watching you itch to tell me, seeing you decide over and over that you needed to guard your little secret. That you were being careful for my sake, not yours. Who else would do that? Really. Not a Sofi, you've seen that. Grace and kindness tag along wherever you go. Now you're gonna have to find something new to be irresistible about. And I'm hungry, so…how about ice cream?"

I wagged *Uh-uh*. I had to tell the egg man he wasn't late at all.

The Ex's Hen Likes Him Easy

His ex-mother-in-law had aphasia, so she often used a peculiar word, one that didn't fit but would lead him toward her meaning. *Flap* meant door, *hole* meant window, *turkey* meant hawk. *Husband* meant son-in-law! That took some getting used to.

Whenever he'd ask whether her daughter had come to visit, she'd say, "I didn't *look at her*." The nurses found this sort of speech either cute or annoying, depending on how hurried they were. But he always found it sweet and funny. "E for effort, Mom! Or should we say S for spunk?" He'd whisper things like this when he'd drop the truck into reverse to leave the facility, keeping Bernice's mind with his, snug as a bug in a *towel*, allowing her warmth to radiate to his own afflicted soul.

New Year's Eve his heart ached, but Bernice had been sanguine. When he wished her good night, she wheeled herself after him, shouting out, "Happy *Easter*!" until two nurses blockaded her chair. And damn it, he would have a happy day tomorrow if only so he'd be able to tell her all about it. He tried to always have a few things bright and amusing to tell her when he came. And to never weep, except for that one time when he needed to let her know about the breakup. It would have been unfair to let her picture things as normal, and who the hell knew when Bernice's daughter would tell her about it or even stop in to visit her?

The holiday had to include something to make for a true and cheerful answer when she'd ask, "Are you *easy?*" He'd take himself to Sissel's Knob. Bernice had always been a tireless hiker and crazy about nature, even in winter, so it was a lock that she'd follow along when he'd tell his story. He was going to sit for a while on the snowy bench at the overlook he calls Misery Point, where so many times he had reflected on the demise and later on the scraps that remained for him to assemble into a future. Where he had told his next-door neighbor, closest friend, on a hike just weeks after the sudden vacuum had been drawn, "You been my Florence Fuckin' Nightingale, bud."

Something would happen at The Knob.

A sick raccoon lying on the trail. You don't have to be a human to hurt so bad you don't give a shit if anybody sees you.

A whitetail could jump right over your head. Any creature can spook.

Of course, the coyotes track and watch, even though you don't bring anything in, not even a granola bar with its package intact. Everything's got an appetite.

That's where he'd go. Bernice would love hearing about the trek. He saw it. Sometime during his story, she'd grab his chin. She always does. He'd smell the feces under her fingernails, and she'd say, "Very bad!" if he has stubble. Or "You like?" if he's clean shaven. But she'd listen.

New Year's morning lit upon him early, and he welcomed that. On his shuffle through the kitchen, he didn't touch the coffee maker. He was minding the voice between his ears.

Wrap the leftover pizza slice in a paper towel. Slip it into your anorak. And there were two more things to do right. One, palm on the gearshift, almost ready. Two, whisper to the windshield, "Awesome day for a *march* in the woods. There'll be plenty for the two us to *sing* about tonight."

One for Hope

Griselda winced when each front tire hopped the lip into Juanita's driveway and it made the most recent eight pounds on her menopausal gut shift. She knew she could be better prepared, for any trip, but especially for one whose real purpose was still a mystery to her. And perhaps she should have been a better friend to Juanita than to have asked her along.

It had been hard to press beyond an Our Father and then a Hail Mary for faith and another one for hope, and here the trip was already upon her. She whisked her beads off her lap and slid them into the glove box of the big conversion van. At some point in the trip, though, Juanita would surely open the glove box. It wouldn't be a big problem if she saw that Griselda had been praying, but *let's don't give Juanita a reason to worry*. So she fished the beads out and walked all the way to the rear to drop them into the jack compartment. On the way, she had bonked her head where the drop ceiling gets lower, and now mumbled curses at herself for not paying attention and for having asked too few questions when she'd had the chance.

Had Roberto allowed her more time to plan, she may have been able to get her father's little car to a shop, then let tall Juanita choose, car or big van. Yet no one had driven the car in nearly a year. Who knows what kind of work it needed. And would it be wise, really, to let Juanita decide anything? Bossy Ita.

With the sprawl of hometown Redding thinning out to its motels and the squatty industrial parks, Juanita seemed to take the now more diffuse landscape as a cue to stop soothing her best friend and begin pestering.

"I don't care what you say, dear. Something is not right. Does Roberto need help? Is he sick?"

"No, Ita," Griselda said. "I think Beto is fine, okay?"

"Your son belongs to both of us. Don't make me say so again. Now I want to see something from you besides this crumpled up map, like you don't know how to get us to San Francisco. Maybe some of his investments are going bad?"

"Enough," Griselda huffed, with more finality than she intended, but what a long three more hours on the road it would be, and at least this worked. Ita's mouth went quiet. But Griselda's mind did not. She knew it wasn't fair to act like Ita had no right to be concerned, after all that this faithful friend had done for Beto throughout the years.

A few more miles slipped by. Griselda remembered the mood rings and other nice trinkets Ita had won for him at the carnival when he was only eight, his whole life still ahead. It was coming back to Griselda, the way he kept saying no, that he wouldn't let Griselda put the rings in her purse for safe keeping. Maybe he thought Tia Juanita wouldn't like that. Maybe he couldn't hear his mother well enough over the snaps and hisses from booths all around. Carnival noises. Happy sounds, unless you really have to concentrate on something.

Maybe Beto is having trouble keeping his focus. So much clatter in that city. *Let him say. Don't try to drag it out of him.*

The City By the Bay did not budge when the van pushed past its welcome billboard. Its buildings stood vertical. The wispy early-November sky did not darken. Not so much as a sheet of newsprint blew across the pavement. And Ita's swishing the Twizzler around in her mouth made no detectable flinch. These had to be good manifestations, from God. His way of saying *Shhhh, Gris. Everything will be fine, okay?*

On the last cell call, Roberto said meet him in the street, parking is *atro-cious.*

Roberto climbed in effortlessly, though his weight rocked the van a little.

"Mi hijo!" Griselda shouted with such joy that it sounded almost like surprise. "Beto, ten months now you're here and I do not see your place."

"You see my face, Mama."

That was so true. A glance to the rearview confirmed it and immediately dropped Griselda into a white space that had no borders, no sharp edges. A space so instantly placid that *Turn left here* almost fell out of it before she could follow his direction.

There was plenty of face time at the Hunan restaurant, so much in fact to be too much without why-are-we-here revealed or even suggested. How are Beto's investments going, has he thought about hiring into an actual investment firm, and what's new back in Redding danced around the gorilla at the table. Roberto twice asked Yuan to bring a new little kettle of hot tea. Ultimately Juanita, who had been pouring and pouring from it, excused herself. Roberto slapped a fifty to the table and summoned Yuan with such impatience that the good waiter had to profusely apologize to the table he'd been tending.

"Please tell the good woman when she comes out, we will be back. Not more than fifteen minutes."

Beto clenched his mother's elbow to hustle her out. He guided her several doors to the left, down a short flight of flagstone steps and into a musty shop overstocked with gardening books and yard ornaments. Still in hustle mode, Griselda overshot how far inside they needed to go for privacy. She bumped a porcelain figurine, an angel whose outstretched hand was shielding a frog from implied rain.

"You should not have brought her, Ma. That was loco."

"Ita is like family, and you…you don't tell me anything."

"Alright, now I will tell you that you have to come back before Thursday, make another trip here." He said Thursday his friend and colleague Matthew was to be back from a weeklong business trip. Griselda's assignment was to take this Matthew's young girlfriend to Redding and put her up in the apartment above the garage, where Grandpa had lived. The evasion throughout lunch had now given way like a levee in rupture. All things became clear, none more than that the girl's life may depend on all of this working quickly and privately, with even Juanita remaining unaware of it. Well, she could realize it gradually in the coming weeks by bits and pieces. The main thing was that the beatings of that sweet girl from Alabama must stop. She had come to Frisco for no other reason than to get away from her father who'd been touching her and her mother who was a foggy drunk, just to end up with the abusive Matthew. *Now* was the perfect time to move her. "You do see this, don't you, Mama?"

Griselda's eyes filled. She cupped her son's head much like the angel for the frog. She rested her other palm on his chest. His pure goodness was never in question, she told him in a hush. There was now only how to get it done. She never even thought to ask how long the girl should be sheltered behind the house. "I cannot come back," she said. "Juanita will know something is up. She will torment me all the way home today as it is, and she would know, if I would come back here. She calls me always, at least twice every day. Could be three, four times."

"You sure messed things up," Roberto said.

"But why didn't you tell me all this when you called?"

"Ma, okay, maybe I should have. You have to make this work though. Mostly, don't let Juanita ask questions, keep interrupting her if you have to. Carlette will be taken care of—I already opened a Redding bank account for her and she has the password. Look, whenever you get to feeling curious, just…God, just…let it go, and make Juanita shut up! I can't believe this."

Griselda felt sorry for *herself*, as if she were a big sister she never had, one who was at her side and able to recognize her melancholy.

On the way to retrieve Ita, her thoughts drifted. She flashed way back, on the fireman in the cherry picker wrapping his arms around little Beto to pull him out of the huge old valley oak behind the garage. On how her precious boy had gripped the fireman's slicker so hard that, when she pulled Beto to her chest, the collar knocked the helmet right off the fireman's head.

Under the restaurant awning, Griselda recalled her son's grasp on her arm from a quarter-hour ago and it reminded her of his death grip on the fireman, his savior. Now *this* situation cried out for a savior. Not for this Carlette girl like Beto had said. Griselda needed to resolve and pretend that she would be saving Beto from the urgency that made his pure goodness stand out so clearly for his mother to see.

The van was double-parked outside Roberto's apartment building, but Griselda was determined to not rush Carlette. The young girl had nothing but two leather travel bags and a bronze lamp with a dazzling stained-glass shade, and Roberto loaded it all within a minute of when Carlette had met them at the curb. He was explaining to the girl how important it was that she was leaving no trail but also must not have any connection back to her danger.

Griselda realized that this was her first chance to study Carlette. How this girl could have the hands and teeth of a fifteen year-old but the manner and voice of twenty was so great a mystery that it would have to wait. Griselda would probe, with patience and sensitivity, over time. On a wrong assumption, she might provide not quite the type of home life Carlette needed. Failing Beto in this way would break Griselda's lonesome change-of-life heart. Where to start probing was a dilemma. A good first question was how old this Matthew friend himself is, but *no*, then again it was not, according to the doubts that flooded over her whenever she'd felt the urge to ask things like that.

On the ride home, Juanita repeatedly poked at Carlette, particularly about her parents, why they had come to be so distant to be *not* the ones shuttling her to a better place. It turned out a strange blessing how many times the girl wanted to stop and get out to smoke. This would knock Juanita off of her interrogation and straight onto how detrimental, unattractive, or downright smelly the cigarette habit is and always will be; how they must have taught Carlette all about that in high school, even in Alabama.

"And by the way, where in Alabama? I never heard of that city, did you, Griselda?"

Griselda was helping unpack her clothes, even before they would make the bed.

"Show me downtown?" Carlette asked.

"Oh sweetheart, you won't need anything from there. We have strip malls. Lots of them."

"Well, is there a bus to downtown?"

"We will try to get Grandpa's car running for you. Don't think about public transportation, okay? It's not so nice anyway."

"I can take care of myself."

"You can even *walk* to the bank where Roberto started your account. I'll draw a little map how to get there. Everything you need is close by us here."

"I swear, Mrs. G, I can take care of myself."

Griselda showed her that the toilet will sing if you don't pull the lever all the way back up and stressed that the water bill is very high. She promised that soon they'll go slipper shopping because "the darned floor gets so cold."

This is not my child was in her head the whole time. *Stop babying her.*

Griselda's slathering of attention really may have begun to annoy Carlette, whose arm was deep in the purse, jabbing and pawing for something. An excuse was what Griselda needed, a reason to go away and let the girl settle in, one that would seem sensible but sweet too. The kitchen stuff. Easing backward, she groped for the door. "I know you won't be cooking right away. In fact, I want you coming to the house to eat, because this whole place is your home now. But I am going to bring back Grandpa's dishes and his silverware. Pots and pans."

Off she was to get those, but she did pause for a second to add, without turning around, "I guess I should tell you too, Grandpa did not die *here*. He loved this place."

The clatter in the purse stopped.

This new quiet made it sound like Griselda shut the door too hard, possibly aggravated, but Carlette may not have heard it that way.

Don't apologize. Just go.

Griselda pulled the last dish from the drainer, stepped into the living room to dry it. This one was a saucer. She would use it to stack some of the candies sitting loose in the Dia de los Muertos altar on the buffet. Why she hadn't thought of this when she set up the altar, she didn't know, but it sorely hurt that she hadn't. This was the first November since her father had died. She turned the wooden rocker to face the altar and just sat, the saucer resting on the towel in her lap. She raised her fingers into a mask over her nose and her mouth, a mask of shame layered on sorrow. Her own voice woke her back to normal. *It's only a dish.* She turned the saucer over, recalling the small and tender disagreement, one of the very few they had ever had. It was a day last summer when he had asked to use the Sharpie so he could write his name on the back of every dish, and then no one breaking into his apartment would want to steal them. Of course it was reasonable to talk him out of that, and part of her job in those tough days was to be a voice of reason.

But now she came to realize that this was just another thing, like the mud on his shoes, like the so-many bottles of pills and his almost daily doctor appointments, all of whose urgency dropped away with such a thud on the day he passed. Had she let him have the Sharpie, she'd have been looking at his name now, seeing his handwriting, remembering how passionate he always was about protecting what he loved; not just his dishes, but Beto and her, above all.

She rose, strode to the junk drawer in the kitchen, found the Sharpie still there. On the overturned saucer, she penned, slowly and deliberately, *Papi, our Beto is a good good Man!*

She thought that maybe tonight, if she's super lucky, she could have the dream again, the one she had when he was only three weeks gone, when she had boxed the last of his things a bit after midnight and fallen into deep sleep from the moment her head hit the pillow. The dream where she walked arm-in-arm with him, down a lane somewhere in Heaven; the one in which, whenever he spoke, it came out as a song.

Back at the altar, she arranged candies on the saucer. Soon enough it would be dusk, so she took the lighter from the drawer and fired the candles, all of them. Now able to whisper what she wasn't ready to before, *That's just nice, isn't it, Papi? It's like I'm there with you.*

A car horn pierced the neighborhood atmosphere. On a scoot to the side window of the living room, Griselda knocked the brass bowl with the ivy off the pedestal, caught the bowl but not the ivy. She saw Carlette in the driveway stooping into a taxi. The double-hung was stuck, so she raced to the front door and across the lawn to stop the taxi, if she could, and Carlette did open the door halfway.

"Mrs. G, don't worry—I'll be back later. And don't tell Roberto." She made a wave to the driver, who zipped straight and fast in reverse. Beyond the curb, Carlette eased her window down and hollered, "What were you gonna do with that bowl?" but gave the driver another wave and didn't wait for an answer.

Griselda ran one more time, now to get her phone. She would call Roberto. This would be within bounds, of course, since now it was certain that he'd given Carlette some rules or instructions. But she paused, just like when she was going to call Beto's dad home from work to chide their son about climbing the valley oak. He would have beaten the boy. That would have been so wrong, especially since little Roberto told her that the only reason he'd climbed the tree was to make her proud of him, that all he ever wants is to make her proud. Beto would later say the same thing about the wealth from his burgeoning career as a broker, and he really means these things. "Just, you must do this in the right ways," she told him, and then immediately wondered whether that correction had been unnecessarily harsh. *Think, Griselda. Good intentions are never enough. Our Heavenly Father and the Blessed Mother will always reveal the best path.* This is how it came to her that, yes, she did need to call someone, but it was Father Madera she should be calling. After Ita, first Ita.

And that call didn't take long. It was almost like Juanita had expected to hear the girl vanished.

The call to Father Madera, though, was taking forever to get through. Griselda was determined to not leave a message, because this matter was too important. When he finally answered, he said through an unmistakable grin, "I've been expecting to hear from you. Juanita has been filling me in. This is hot news, right? You would think Our Lady of Fatima had arrived in this town, it's such a lovely buzz." Everything was *lovely* to the good priest.

"I want to get Carlette involved in the parish," Griselda told him.

"Mmm, first we find out what we've got here. You see, she took the taxi to downtown. Juanita told me all about it. Griselda, volunteering is to help the needy, it's not to keep volunteers out of trouble. You know my assistant, Father Lucas, right? And that he heads up our volunteer network?"

"Of course."

"Well, he will figure this out. He knows all about drugs, in case that's it. He even knows how to talk Street. Boy, our Juanita, she really is something, isn't she? You're lucky to have such a friend, I tell you."

Father Lucas, whom Father Madera had dispatched to the house before daybreak, was snoring in the recliner when Juanita creaked the front door open. Griselda motioned for her to come softly to the kitchen, but the priest was already stirring by then and rubbing his face, and he followed Juanita—she upright and steady—he lumbering behind. Juanita gave a pinch to Griselda's earlobe before each of them took a seat at the table, which had been set since seven o'clock, shortly after Father arrived.

Now he sat scheming with the two women, as if they all were plotting an elaborate robbery. He would take the girl for a long hike, get her worn out. She would let her guard down. On the bridge, before the river trail, Juanita would peel off at the sundial and say that she'll meet back up with them there around sunset. She told Father this will be hard, because deception is not natural to her. He told her there was nothing dishonest about it. She was simply taking a break to do the few errands that he had just helped her think of. He said to look at it this way: when *God* doesn't tell us everything, is He deceiving us? She conceded that God could never deceive. But doesn't He love us so much, Father Lucas asked her, that He waits until we are ready to find things out?

What time did Carlette get in, Juanita insisted on knowing. 3:08 this morning, Griselda reported. And what have we got now, the priest wondered. Almost eleven, Juanita told him. When to wake the girl was getting too complicated. Finally Father pointed out that this was *breakfast, not an intervention*, and their tension unraveled into a giggle. Griselda examined this relief, though, while she was laughing. She was unsure what was expected of her. This was how she might feel if a close friend handed her a special thing to admire without saying whether it was a gift to her. But Father could now roll forth a plan.

He clapped once, they all stood up and sprang into it. Griselda led up the steps along the garage wall with Juanita in her shadow and then Father Lucas, who would wait just outside for some indication. When Carlette didn't acknowledge the taps on the apartment door, Griselda allowed herself to go in anyway. The whole distance to the bed, she maintained a cadence of *Carlette, Carlette* until the girl stretched and hummed an *Mmm-hmm*. Behind Griselda, Juanita reacted with a firm, businesslike, "Well, good," and left the apartment to take the priest back to the kitchen.

Griselda told Carlette, "We're going to have breakfast together, darling, and we have someone, someone delightful for you to meet. Can you shower? Or just freshen up and come down?"

The girl yawned and unfolded her arms out to a fisted V, which gave Griselda the chance to see bruises. In the swath of sun pouring in through the side window, she was even able to read where a thumb and fingers had clamped into the girl's upper arm to make those.

"Okay," Carlette said, "breakfast sounds nice." She relaxed one fist and offered that hand for something. Griselda met it with her own, and Carlette squeezed hard and long while wiggling to sit up. She kept that grip until she needed the hand to retrieve the silk spaghetti strap that had fallen from her shoulder.

It was time for the three to head out for their long walk. Father Lucas let Juanita and Carlette into his car, then came back up to the house to get his sunglasses, which he said he'd forgotten.

"Look for us around six," he said. "Everything's up in the air, but we'll know a lot more."

"Some Matthew in San Francisco was hurting her," Griselda told him. "I have seen her bruises so plain."

"Gotta go."

The only thing Griselda felt needed figuring out was why everyone else was convinced there was more to the story.

She made use of the others' hike time searching the web for *Matthew* and *broker* and *San Francisco*, checking ten pages of results. Twice she picked up her phone to call Beto to ask about this Matthew character, but each time abandoned that thought as she heard his words play back, that it would be best for Carlette if they keep him out of the picture, to give it at least two or three weeks for her to get adjusted before anybody contacts Roberto. Griselda resigned herself to the notion that Father Lucas was going to get the scoop on what Carlette had been doing last night, and in a few moments aside tonight, he would explain it to the two ladies. And tell them about the volunteer opportunities too.

The house came abruptly alive with Carlette, Juanita, and Father Lucas all filing in from their get-acquainted walk on the river trail, remarkably close to Father's projected time. Carlette marched straight through, like the house were just an entry hall for the back yard and garage.

"I wanna get cleaned up. Oh, Mrs. G, that area by the river is awesome; well, they'll tell you. I mean, they'll tell you how much *I* liked it." The bare kitchen walls still rang with her joy after she was out the back door.

Juanita also breezed by Griselda, put a couple bags of new groceries on the counter and opened the refrigerator.

"How did it *go?*" Griselda asked her. "What did she say about this Matthew? Does she feel safe here?"

"Why didn't you answer?" Juanita said. "I left three messages. Where is your cell? Go get it."

"It didn't ring."

"Go get it now."

Griselda whirled on both heels. When she returned from her computer room, she held her lit phone, palm up, right under Ita's face. "See? No messages."

Juanita took it from her. "Let me look at this," she said, and drifted into the living room. "You get the cold things put away."

Gris was slow to obey, slow enough to still be there when Father Lucas popped back in carrying a big soft suitcase, which he set at Juanita's feet.

He made a declaration. "We feel it's best for Juanita to stay with you for a few days. She will be of great help."

Celery. Pork chops. Butter. Griselda shut the fridge. She felt ready. But vaguely perplexed. *I must make it be okay if they will talk to me all night. This is worth it!* She took a seat in the living room. "There were no calls, no messages," she said to Ita. "Give me the phone. You saw, right?"

"So sorry you weren't able to join us," Father Lucas said, "but it could have been much too strenuous."

"I want to know all about this Matthew person. Why was she with him? Did he *ever* treat her good? Also…you know…the other *point* of your walk: what she can get into at the parish. Is there something she wants to do?"

Juanita pointed at the priest.

"The church needs to back away from this," he said. "We can possibly do something later for the girl, depending. But Griselda, this kind of thing is not for us, except to bring in the right people."

"That girl *has* the right people," Griselda said. "Me. As long as this Matthew does not come up to bother her, she will be fine."

"Griselda, my dear——" Juanita started.

"We believe there is no Matthew," Father said.

"Are you crazy?" Griselda shouted. She jerked not only herself, but her brocado chair by its arms too, so both would squarely face Ita. "You didn't see the marks because of her sweatshirt, but you know I saw them."

"The bruises on her arms," Juanita said, "those are red. If some Matthew made them, they would be blue or brown by now."

"Then who? Who? Oh no, my baby did not do that. You're both crazy. You are. You're crazy…Let's say you're right, and you're not! Why would he send her up here if he was rough with her? Besides, she is way too young for him. And when I saw them together, it was clear, so clear, they were never a couple. She's practically a child, for God's sakes." Griselda felt a hot rush of shame at her own rage, then sober in her logical defense of her son. But her eyes glossed. "Give me my phone. I'm calling Beto. You'll see."

"Griselda. Griselda, we must prevent you, for your own good," Father said.

"From talking to my son? What kind of priest are you?"

"A very, very sad one. Griselda, we do not suspect Beto has been rough with her, but, and I wish this was all, Carlette is sixteen and she is a runaway."

"What do you mean, *I wish this was all?*"

Father Lucas sighed. "Roberto's first encounter with Carlette was at the airport," he said. "Middle of April. She literally bumped into him on the escalator. That's what she does, because that way they can smell her perfume. He said he had to meet somebody from New York and he gave her the brush-off, but Carlette decided to trail him from a distance anyway. She saw him meet up with some guy who had flown in, then followed the two of them to a hotel shuttle. She waited a few minutes and got on the same bus. Your son looked like he didn't think much about that. In the lobby, she watches the floor number above his elevator. She kills a little time, then walks up to that floor and waits in a little nook. Maybe twenty minutes later, Roberto comes out with his briefcase and goes to the elevator. Right before it pings at his floor, Carlette knocks on the same suite. She doesn't care that he sees her. He mutters, *What the hell is this?* He shakes his head and then he gets on the elevator and he's gone."

"That's my boy. You would like him."

"A few days later Roberto calls up Carlette."

"He took her number?" Griselda said.

"No. Here's what he later told Carlette: the guy who had flown in was in Finance and he was there to interview people. When he called Roberto to say thanks for your interest but you didn't get the job, he thanked him for sending Carlette."

"But he didn't send her," Griselda pointed out.

"Right. There'll be no argument about that. Anyway, back to when she knocked on the guy's door...Carlette said to the guy that the other fellow, she was talking about Roberto, had told her the guy was from New York and she was just wondering, was he lonely? Would it make him feel better if they spent a little time together? He let her in."

"So what? My boy did nothing, and you agree. Say it!"

"Well, when the guy called him, Roberto told the guy he lost Carlette's number and did *he* have it? Then Roberto calls Carlette, tells her how he got her number and says he can set her up with a nice place and steady clients, classy like that, the Finance type. Get her away from the airport where she could get arrested. He would take a *slice of the pie.*"

"No way. Uh-uh, Father."

"The *nice place* was Roberto's apartment, and he kept her very busy. The authorities will look for an appointment book here, maybe names or notes. Perhaps handwritten room numbers, possibly even something threatening-sounding from Roberto, that could have fallen out of Carlette's purse or she tucked somewhere, who knows. Something like this may be in your father's apartment right now, but they'll look everywhere."

Griselda waved away the priest's words. "There is no such thing!" she screamed out. She glared at Juanita, who deflected it to Father Lucas, who in turn was wearing his dread with his head atilt, looking through his lashes toward the air above Griselda. None of this was possible. The girl had gone for a hike with a priest and Griselda's best friend. A hike. They had to have seen how delicate she is. She was almost still a child. They didn't see Carlette squeeze Gris's hand, the innocence. They couldn't know anything. "*Someone* has been rough with her! You ignore this while you make stuff up. I bet she never said half of it. Big shot detectives, the two of you, like on TV."

"Griselda, I know this is hard to hear," Father Lucas said, "but it's not hard to see. Listen up now. She doesn't know how long Roberto is going to be pumping money into her account, so she's actually smart to think it won't be for long. So the first night she's here, she's out doing the only thing she knows to do when she gets to a new city. And the men who accept her offer, well, those are not gentlemen."

Juanita jumped in. "Gris, Beto was watching the news one night. He sees they're cracking down on child prostitution. It's a big investigation, the whole Bay Area."

"See, to Roberto, just stopping won't be enough," Father continued. "He's got to get rid of Carlette. He can't send her to Alabama because her parents would find out about him, and he wouldn't know *when* they find out."

Griselda corrected him. "Carlette does not talk to them. They were abusing her."

"No, they weren't, and Roberto knows they're good people. He knows they would make her tell everything. So up here, there's your father's apartment and, just as important, there's you."

"Beto is sure *you* would let him know if she starts blabbing," Juanita said. "Then he would disappear. He wouldn't say so to you, he would just be gone. This is what I think."

Griselda pounded her own knee. "No one cares what you think!" But she sobbed. She was using her palms to blot the tears, so Juanita made for the buffet to get her tissues. Griselda jumped out of the chair, shoved her from behind, sending Juanita's shoulder into the altar, where the frame with Griselda's father's picture collapsed and crashed to the floor. Chocolate skulls fell too, and they bounced like the fat first raindrops of a midsummer storm.

Juanita regained her posture and said, "Thank goodness the candles are all right."

Father Lucas looked at Juanita with what appeared to be a question so well-rehearsed that he didn't need to vocalize it. She threw a glance to the kitchen clock, then drew with her index finger on her chest a quarter circle, top to right. Father nodded, and Juanita stalked like a soldier right past Griselda, through the kitchen and out the back.

From the floor, rounding up the offerings, Griselda shot daggers at Father Lucas.

He only opened both palms, like what else could he have done?

She said, "You are nothing. How dare you? You have been reading too much newspaper."

"They're going to ask lots of questions and the less you hear from me, the better. Maybe that's been too much already. God will be at your side, Griselda. He tries us, but He never leaves us. We just all need to be truthful."

The furnace kicked on. The priest looked a bit startled by it. He pushed himself up from the loveseat to offer his hand. "*This* could be of some comfort. My own father—"

"Stop!" Griselda yelled. But her vengeance evaporated and left her only vacant.

Carlette was the first into the back door. She must have noticed the table wasn't set and the kitchen didn't smell of food. So she asked, would they be ordering out? No one answered, so she scanned the rooms for Griselda's face. Found it and read it. Carlette pulled her shoulders in. Fear seized her. Unquestionably fear.

"What? What? I didn't do anything," she said, and then turned to Father Lucas. "Everything out there was between the two of us!" But her steely forehead softened in disbelief. "I trusted you."

He stood like a man who has set fire to a pile of leaves and is biding time, silently watching it smolder until it can handle more.

"I can't go home," Carlette whimpered. "I'll go back to Roberto's, but I can't go home. I won't."

"We think you won't have a choice," Juanita said from behind Carlette.

Griselda lunged toward Juanita, but Father Lucas from behind crimped into both her shoulders. So she screamed over Carlette's head, "Shut up. You are…dirt!"

"How could you do this to me?" Carlette whimpered to Griselda. "What kind of a mother are you?"

The front door grunted like a person who is trying to interrupt, so all of them turned full attention to it. Father Madera was on the threshold. Behind him on the front porch, three stout men and a woman, all in dark jackets, waited.

It's not like Father Lucas hadn't told Griselda what to expect. The idling cars seemed, at last, near ready to roll. One of the men was stretching the last length of yellow tape to span the newels at the base of the front steps. Griselda turned herself around to watch, out the rear window. The kind one, who had jumped out to go back—past the car where Father Lucas, Carlette, and Juanita sat—was returning from the tow truck that had her van on its hitch. The car door at her elbow clunked open, and he let the beads slither into her palm. He shut it, but not before whispering, "Like we said, it's only questions. We might be able to get you back here yet tonight. Can't promise."

Griselda gaped at her property. All the lights were still on in Grandpa's apartment. In the house, all the first-floor lights including the front porch lamps were still ablaze. So were the point lights that illuminate the back yard and the face of the garage. The gigantic valley oak stood over it all, plain as in the noonday sun, trying so hard to still look proud. She knew now, she'll never have it cut down. Never.

The Reminder

I had let brandy, of all things, pass through my throat just to see what could happen with the redhead. She did rest her hand on my thigh, about an inch-an-a-half from my stuff. But why did I let her hang on me that night?

I thought I was fairly good looking, worthy of the attention she was slathering on me. It had to do with the way my hair obeys in the wintertime and the new pima shirt that sat just right on my shoulders and cuffed out exactly where my knobby wrists wanted it to.

And there was one other thing that made the blur from all that brandy such a welcome lens—my pre-law classes weren't going exceedingly well. As a young man, I was very much of a mind that I should learn whatever I wanted to learn and ignore the rest. This was a phase, but I had not yet outgrown the notion that it was a trademark. I made no bones about the difficulties with school, even told the bartender, who had no cause to care. So the only reason telling him makes any sense is that this was one of those personal facts one tosses to the world to prove how open and honest he is.

Veronica, whom I'd often referred to in those days as a godsend, had yelled at me that afternoon for a shameful indiscretion she was right about. Still, these were not reasons for drinking; I drank for a single reason—the constitutional inability to resist the lure of alcohol. The jury is still out on this, but sobriety does feel a lot like coming home, and it's so good to be home.

Being an orphan, boohoo. Being in hock for my education, oh well. These were not reasons.

I can still hear the bartender knocking the bottom of my glass against the bar, twice, and saying, "I guess that'll be it."

At that point, I leaned toward the redhead and mumbled, "Maybe some other night *what?*"

But she was already gone, her coat, her purse, everything. Her leggings. Her clever lips.

I slapped the cash down, too much I'm sure, and gave my best rendition of an okay me in a wobble toward the door. I deliberately yawned to try to convince the good man, whose back was already toward me and whose mind was fixed on his register tallies, that I was only tired. It made him glance over his shoulder, though, and when he did, he hollered out, didn't I want that white lighter I left on the bar? No, I didn't, but the okay me thought I should go back and get it, because that's what a sober guy would do.

A sober guy wouldn't have even bought it. The redhead smoked Marlboro golds. When she had drifted out the first time to have one, I jogged across to the quick stop and bought the lighter so I could be the gentleman who would fire up all of her next ones. White I picked for gallantry, white knight. It got a lot of use. There's something in how a woman caresses your hands when you light her cigarette, especially when there's no wind blowing. It gives a man the sensation of being appreciated, and that's never been a small thing to me.

A fresh layer of snow on the parking lot surprised me, and I slid around and flailed like Scotty Hamilton on steroids. This ineptitude must have shaken me, because I sat with a gratitude grip on the steering wheel for as long as it took the defroster to clear the windows, and then I continued to sit a while. I remembered having told the redhead, whose name I now couldn't retrieve, we could build a fire at my place, how nice that would be. She made a peaceable groan, like the purr of a well-fed cat, and took another sip of her brandy Manhattan.

So, now alone, I was trying to dial up a picture of whether I'd like a fire when I got home. On this I waffled plenty. Some of the wood was not sheltered, so it would have to wait till I'd have invincible embers. But a fire in the hearth would be nice. On the other hand, if Veronica came over unannounced, she might wonder why I had a fire going for only me. But that wouldn't tell her anything about the redhead. As in many ardently fought debates, I can't recall the winning argument for all the convincing blows landed before it. But home was the only destination, and operating the truck was easier than I'd feared.

Sometimes you get a little gift like that, the unexpected skill, and begin to contemplate what it might have been a bennie for. Was it for good behavior, for not taking the redhead home, at least for not taking her home without telling her about Veronica? Was it for not arguing back, for letting Veronica's verbal punches hit me without hoping she'd feel guilty for throwing them? Or was it a positive sign about me, an indication that my self-assessments are conservative, that I'm prone to think I'm drunker than I really am, and this will serve quite well in a future of marginal alcohol abuse? My competence to drive was a gift in any case.

But like a nail without a hammer, it stopped being of use when the engine power fell in a gradual taper. I recognized this as fuel pump failure and pulled to the only length of shoulder available, which was short, but long enough for me get the whole truck off the road before it died. I turned lucid.

Still six miles from home, I wasn't going to get there by walking. But I couldn't stick with the truck, intoxicated like I was. There was no taxi service in town. There certainly were a few near the U, but they wouldn't come all the way out here, I knew. I would have to appeal to someone to drive me. I'd start walking, get away from the truck first, then thumb.

I got a couple hundred yards and realized, if I'm carrying my keys and I'm wasted, and my truck is a little ways back, this constitutes proof that I had been driving drunk. So I went *all the way back* to put the keys in the ignition.

The second time I reached the sharp-left-curve sign where I'd had the epiphany about the keys, it dawned on me, my house keys were still on the ring, dangling from the ignition. This was tough, very tough. To believe, as I did—when you experience luck, a meter starts to run and, yes, ultimately you will run out of luck—I just knew going back a second time posed more than twice the risk of a DUI.

I went anyway. But for the first time all night, I trembled, all the way back. This is why I was so glad that a van stopped to pick me up pretty soon after I grabbed my house keys. I might skate, I thought, and then I laughed at the recollection of how I'd already skated. In the bar's parking lot. *Just call me Scotty*, I whispered, right before I climbed in.

I could smell the weed. These folks in the van seemed to be tying a good one on of their own, and *More power to 'em*, I thought. They had given me the seat by the sliding door. The driver was Dale, who smoked, one after the other, what looked like shorty unfiltered cigarettes. He introduced his girlfriend Marta, who rode shotgun and his kid brother Eric, who was in the captain chair next to mine. There was something not right with Eric. I could tell by the way he kept grinning and laughing too long after each thing this group found amusing. His face looked a little off, too, although in the dark interior I couldn't tell in what way. But then, who was I to think that somebody else looked a little off?

Then I found out they were on a mission. We were? They were headed for Dale's brother's house. His brother was out of town on business. Dale's sister-in-law was having an affair. If the *asshole* was there, they would make him regret the whole intrigue. If he wasn't, they would make the sister-in-law abandon it. With every little detail Dale shared, Marta would half turn her face toward the back and smile. This made the sinister disclosure oddly agreeable to me, though of course it shouldn't have.

There was something in that smile. Marta was not beautiful or even necessarily pretty. I had just never known a woman so possessed of the capacity to be okay with everything around her. I made up in my mind—because I really thought I saw it—that had she been in charge, she never would have devised this brash visit, and if someone else suggested it, she'd have decisively nixed it. But not being in charge and understanding she wasn't, she could be at peace, even find the funny in the terribly unfunny. As if this weren't strange enough, it was stranger yet that I found this almost unbearably attractive in her. And this is the only reason I can think of for why I didn't protest when Dale crossed my highway without so much as touching the brakes, even after I said, "Hey, guys?"

I did try again to get home without becoming an accomplice to the scheme that so likely would have a bad end. I remember thinking, *They resonate to silliness*, so I deployed a measure of it. "As your lawyer, and yours and yours, let me explain something about tort law. Dale, you be the…party of the first part. No, the second part." Marta loved it. My legal nonsense triggered her sense of humor to dance, which further charmed me. She teased, "First part," and shoved Dale's shoulder, then, "No, second part," and did it again, then rested her palm on my knee.

This tenderness roused me into an awakening. The redhead, for all her toying, had not affected me in any similar way. And, given that these happened on the same night, I trusted the sampling and thus imputed to Marta an eerie power to move me. When I drank, I tended to treasure and exaggerate nearly *all* things for how amorous they made me feel. So I generously credited her with many other abilities she hadn't demonstrated and that weren't logically associated with anything but the space Veronica had vacated by way of her tirade. Marta was now my conductor and the train had left the station. And I, having trusted Marta, saw myself trusting, by extension, this whole bunch.

When she and Dale began to whisper to each other, I thought they were amused with me, so I poured it on. "Your

Honor, may my clients have a moment to discuss this new turn of events? Of course, thank you, Your Honor."

But this time I'm not sure they heard me. Eric did. He slapped his knee and shouted *Your Honor* three or four times between his guffaws. Dale and Marta didn't react.

Thinking Dale may have been plotting a yet more devious way to blow up his sister-in-law's stasis, I gave goofiness one more litigious shot. "Let us now turn to the constitutional rights of the party of the fourth part. Let us say, for example, she has cookies in the oven."

But this, too, evoked no reaction of any kind from Dale or Marta. Eric started to bounce in his seat, and I found myself shushing him. I was getting either bold or frightened.

Beyond a bluff on our right, the roadway offered a shoulder and Dale pulled off onto it. Before he jumped out, he said he needed to fetch the flashlight from under my seat. I groped for it but couldn't locate it by the time he slid my door open. Marta turned around toward me and whispered, "You'll be all right, honey," and punctuated her assurance with one of those ever-innocent smiles.

Dale grabbed me just above my right elbow and tore me from the van, then hollered over my head, "Eric! Help me out here!" Eric did, and seized my left arm the same way. The two of them dragged me to a barbed-wire fence and threw me over it. From the ground I saw them each in turn, Dale first, Eric mimicking, step on the highest wire and bounce over it into the pasture. This had to be a sheep ranch. I knew roughly where we were, but because I did, I also knew we were tens of miles from help. They dragged me about another football field until, when Dale yelled "Now!" they threw me face down onto the ground. As they did, Dale kicked both legs out from under me, and my shins immediately felt like toothaches.

I didn't try to move at first. The kick had told me they were not just getting rid of me, they were at least willing to risk that I not survive this. So I played as if I lacked the strength to. I lay still and watched them the whole time, at first squinty, then wide-eyed, until they got back into their van and began to drive off. Then I let a few more minutes pass to make sure they weren't coming back to check on me. These minutes I used for regret and then remedial planning. I would walk south, deeper into the pasture, hoping to find either a sheep shelter or a ranch house.

When I finally stirred, I found my right cheek was stuck, frozen to the ground. Nothing I did to try to free my face caused me any pain because my face was numb, but everything about it scared me. Every time I tried, I failed. The force pulling back toward the ground was stronger than I could push away using both elbows and both knees. My fingers were numb too, so to feel around for something, anything, I had to use the top sides of my hands. This turned up a small, detached clump of sage florets about the size of a baseball, but I resisted the impulse to think of it as a miraculous find. I just pulled it toward me and pushed it under my neck so a puff of wind wouldn't take it.

I realized I should thank providence for the bartender's extra care—I remembered the lighter in my front pocket. I let a small laugh out at the fleeting thought that maybe the redhead's hand on my thigh was a grope for the lighter and was hinting nothing more than that she wanted to smoke. It dawned on me, right there sprawled on the cold ground, that a sense of humor is a gift, and maybe mine isn't as big as Marta's, but mine could carry me, maybe even all the way out of this dilemma.

I tried hot breath to loosen the hold the ground had on my cheek, but that quickly made it worse. The frozen area broadened. The *whole* side might become stuck and in that case there would be no tearing away, even if I resigned to losing a portion of my face.

It came back, what I'd been thinking about before the hot breath idea. The lighter. Vision would be a problem, as dark as it was, but I had to find a nearby tumbleweed if there was one. This would take contortion, but I knew I had to use each hand in front of my face, which itself had no range to rotate. One hand would operate the lighter, while the other shielded my eyes from its glare.

I was then prepared to declare something as miraculous, because only three or four feet away was a good tumbleweed. I would light the sage and flick it to land under the tumbleweed. Not easy. And utterly final. If it worked, the brush would burst into a modest ball of fire, short-lived but big enough to be seen from some distance if anyone happened to be so near and looking that way. I would wait. Maybe a car would appear. If not, I would hope for the impossible coincidence of some ranch hand having a gander out there, right when the ball ignites.

I found it easy to be on high alert and still reflect on how I got there and how I wanted me to be, if I were lucky enough to get out. My eyes had been adjusting after all, so I studied the walls of the canyon and took note of my position in it, at its bottom. Of course, I acknowledged the stupidity of drinking like a fish. But I also gave remarkable credence to a notion that the little signs of good cheer I'd observed from Marta had a lasting, settling effect on me, and that this may have kept me from altogether giving up. I'm convinced it made me ready and dexterous when headlights did hit the road above me.

The driver was a deputy, who noticed my blazing tumbleweed and hustled down into the pasture. When I was able to hear her boots crunch, I grunted so loud I didn't sound human. I'm not sure why I didn't use words to direct her to me, but I didn't have to. Once there, the good woman took my word for it and didn't try to lift me. She called the fireman she had summoned and asked him to bring down some tools. *Fast, Johnny, fast*, she hollered into her radio. I heard him come back with something garbled, but she answered, *Not vitals, not yet*. It was only minutes before the fireman stood over me with a crowbar and a propane torch. By what I now think of as genius, he alternated punching deeper and deeper holes into the frozen ground near my head and shooting flame into them, doggedly, until the earth relented.

The next morning, dressing to leave the hospital room, I found fragments of shearling from the inside of my jacket in the pocket of my jeans. So retrieving the lighter must have been strenuous, although I recall it feeling like only an exercise of a treasured privilege. These strands now glistened in the light.

Severe frostbite had claimed a large patch of skin from my cheek. The tissue died, forever, in the shape of an upside-down pear. Several doctors and even more friends over the years have prodded me to have a graft procedure to fix it, but I'm still finding it easy to dismiss the urge to the have that done. When the persistent ones ask why, I usually tell them I don't know, and that's mostly true. I walk away from their question thinking, though, that this scar is as much a part of me as any feature I carry from earlier in life. I've fancied it like a peculiar badge of honor, even though I don't see anything honorable in my behavior of that night. I'll tell strangers it's a birthmark. Sometimes because I don't feel like explaining. More often because their thoughts about my regard for it really don't matter to me.

Eventually my future landed, like a balloon losing air, in homeowners insurance as an adjuster, where claimants have tended to find me a pushover as I always initially apply the reckless assumption that they're telling me the truth. Yet I'm at ease with this because they *live* their realities, and I only offer possibilities. I just stand beside an imaginary gate while they pass through or don't. So acceptance—I have come to think—is what lights the path to all the essential truths about somebody else; the gnarly, the desperately painted over, and the charming, simply natural. Everything will crawl toward you into that light if you'll stand back and let it.

This I've never read anywhere. Anywhere but between the lines in the tale of my younger life. Mine and Marta's.

Unredeemable

Helen is dozing. Erika the Adult Sunday School teacher is *not* going to like this. A few minutes ago Helen was wrapping her brown-gray hair around her index finger, so I knew this was coming. Bart sees it and he's pissed. But which Mister Clean are you right now, Bart? Just the starchy, scornful bald guy or his Doppelganger, the God-appointed vindictive prison guard type? I won't know till an hour from now, when we've all settled into our big booth at the diner.

The only other one who sees Helen doze, I think, is Al from the Ozarks, whose trademark is to say *I wanna live forever and then turn into somethin' good to eat*. Al kicks my boot, my iguana, come on, because he's sitting next to me and he can and because he's always kicking my boot. It's his special way of communicating. This can mean, like now, *I know what you're thinkin', yessir*, or like other times *I missed it, what?* At the bar it can mean either *Five bucks says this one's got a steady boyfriend*, or just *Hey, gimme a cigarette*. His special but not too specific way of communicating. I dip my right shoulder and whisper at him, "Don't...kick...the lizard." From my angle under these cold glaring lights, I think I see his black beard stir and his prankster mouth curl upward.

The lesson for today is about not looking back like Lot's wife did, but old Helen is about twenty seconds away from turning into a pillar of salt that has its salty finger stuck in its salty hair. It strikes me she would make a great billboard face for welcome to our sleepy little South Dakota town, emphasizing the dreaminess, so when the tourists drive through and see our vacant storefronts—a full seven years into this new century of progress—they'll figure this is just how we want our town to be. *Shhhh. Don't wake us up, please. We're in the middle of a nice long town nap.*

This thought cracks me up enough that I have to cover my grin, which I think I manage to do pretty well. But God gave Erika eyes in the back of her head and the balls to use them, so she's walking backwards (which my dad used to do when he was sick, and it drove me crazy because God didn't give him those extra eyes and he was so bad at it he was a hazard to society), and she's heading straight towards me without skipping a beat in her lesson. Just when Erika's set to whip around and ask me a question she knows I don't care about, Mindy the absolute doll who has two little sons and a tight little marriage—damn it—saves the day by throwing her hand in the air and asking Erika, "How do we understand this thing that happened to Lot's wife, in the light of New Testament forgiveness?"

Al cracks out a single wet bark that amounts to the first hack of a cough his body didn't get the memo about, and Erika just rolls into the answer to Mindy's question, easy as a drunk dropping into bed.

"To understand this, and I'm so glad you brought this up, Mindy, we need to have a multidimensional view of the Trinity. Now many would say that the latter era is characterized by a broadening of God's tolerance for sin and sinners, but we know this to be incorrect. Let me…personalize this explanation.

My daughter LizBeth came home from——" and bang, just then the bell rings to signal us all that the worship service begins in eight minutes, and I can say from experience, the bell's not kidding about the eight minutes. "Next week we'll come back to this," Erika says, and with that she picks up her Bible, notebook, and purse and, except for the tiniest tilt that I thought just might snap the heel off her stiletto, does a pretty damn graceful job of leading us lemmings down the hall, up the stairs, and into the sanctuary.

The diner is clanky with the bus boy shoving dirty dishes into his portable tub, and the blood's rushing to my head because I'm half underneath the table trying to pick up a few macaronis off the floor so nobody skids on those and pulls a groin or worse, and Erika's trying to ask me a question. I guess charm school wasn't for manners. Plus, I chucked my head against the edge of the table on the way down. And her question—this big deal—is "So, Kenny, what would you say was the most important thing in your life a year ago?"

She clearly wasn't listening on the steps after church, when Reverend Bob wouldn't let go of his grip on my hand. He was saying, "Kenny, one day you're going to tell me the Lord has come to live in your heart…Until then, I'm never quite sure if I can jump for joy."

I gave him a wide grin and planted a pretty good left hook on the soft bump of his shoulder. I said, "How 'bout go ahead and jump." Hey, if he's gonna clamp down with his meat hook like that, anything goes.

"Well, I hope you got what you came for," he said, and then he curled up his lips the same way a smiling person does but without showing any teeth, which I don't call a smile.

"Nnn, not yet Reverend Bob. You know I'm only in it for the food."

And man, he loosened his grip right then. I was looking up the steps at the new lady from the Co-op, pretending I thought she was trying to get his attention and that I wanted to let her, which worked. It was either that or my remark about the food, which was only half true, but a darned good half.

So now at the diner I deal with Erika, Reverend Bob Junior—not related, but they're definitely part of that full-court press bunch. "Sorry?" I finally answer, hoping she'll just say never mind.

"A year ago. The most important thing in your life."

I have to think, and then I go with what worked on the steps. "Well, Erika…guess I'd have to say food was right up there."

But she comes right back with "Kenny, just once I'd like you to treat me like a person," and this knocks me for a loop. I'm trying hard to detect some phony thing in how she holds herself, to make sure I didn't really hurt her feelings, but my bullshitometer needle isn't budging. So I open up like I'm going to answer her question in earnest, but when she sees this, she turns her whole body in the booth towards Mindy. Then, as if she's got second thoughts, she glances over her shoulder and tosses one word to me, "Really!" the way somebody might flick a receipt out a car window. So it wasn't acting, I did hurt her feelings. I've got pins sticking into my head. And great, this is all I need, something to remember to have to fix with somebody.

Good thing Al is here. He's 180 from me in this big booth, so he can't reach with his leg to kick me but he comes up with a good one, pinching his beard as if this required some intricate thinking, "How's about some fresh air?" Which, when he and I do go out for a smoke, doesn't make things feel especially better.

Erika is magazine-cover pretty, anybody would tell you that. She's a dee-vor-cee. Now, for someone like that, I don't draw a conclusion about what went haywire in her married life. She's got a forceful way about her alright, but from all my reading, I've pretty much decided that nobody gets a good sense of what pushes couples apart just from noticing a few things about them. Besides, whatever happened to her marriage happened in Nebraska.

There was a time early on, maybe last November, when I wondered what Erika would be like. Then I wondered it out loud to Al at the bar one night. Through a handful of beard came, "Listen, did you ever toss a frisbee in your sandals on a clover meadow? It's like dancin' on air. That's how romance is, right? Are you with me? But some…time, you don't know when but you know it just the same, when you're runnin' to catch that sucker, a honeybee is gonna get in between your toe and your sandal and sting you but good. The bee is Erika, buddy. Just my opinion, of course. No charge this visit." And then he slapped my back, and my mouth must have been open because it made this deep, hollow boom like a Lakota drum. I never after that fancied the notion of Erika being with me.

Outside the diner now, the breeze has that dampness to it where, when it blows your hair out of place, your hair stays there. I think to remind Al about his advice, so I can thank him I guess, but what for? Erika did pout, and it's no way my fault her feelings are hurt, but I still have to fix it and that's not going to happen today.

From the foot of my long P-shaped driveway, the view is like a travelogue. All the hues are more vivid than when I left for church. I'll drive it slow and appreciate the buds, their violets and yellows, and the deep green of the lawn, to catch all these in the act of thriving here, of being mine— all mine—in glorious April. Something really isn't right, though.

Red, my all-time favorite rooster, is strutting like he's trying to solve the problems of the world and he's down to ironing out the final details. Red is usually the coolest temperament around this place. When something's got him stirred up, I better pay attention, so instead of bending to the right and the house, I go straight, toward the shop end of the loop. Nothing concerns me tremendously, but I've got a drum of dumped gas, with the who-knows-how-much two-stroke oil in it, the gas I sell dirt-cheap to the farmers for them to blend with their good gas. This is one of the few side benefits and one of the few hazards of my small engine repair shop. *Small as in small engine, not small shop*, I always say. I don't need some bored teenager burning my not-small shop to the ground. Every once in a while though, Red's a damned liar, and this appears to be the once in a while.

Out of those god-awful dress clothes and having my bolo zipped back into its little baggie where it won't tarnish, I drop myself into the rocker and settle on an article in my *Atlantic*. This one's about where there's wireless access to the Internet in the U.S.A. and where there's not. Nobody knows this about me: I read, a lot. So sometimes this feels like sneaking, like I'm stealing a little knowledge and squirreling it away. Fuck 'em. I'm at the Great Southwest part of the article.

Quick knocks rattle my wooden screen door. It's Reverend Bob in a sky blue crewneck and gray jeans, and more startling, wearing an apologizing look. These people from church, they sure know how to make you let your guard down. "Kenny, I hope it's okay I'm here," he says. "On a Sunday, you know."

"Shoot, I don't mind. Just tell me you're not trying to get me to do any work on this…Most Holiest of All Days of the Week."

"Oh, no. No, I just thought I might *talk* to you about a little bit of work." He motions with his head for me to come out.

I whip my army surplus from the coat tree and do a sloppy job of putting it on since I'm watching to make sure he negotiates my decaying front steps, my someday project. "Well, Reverend Bob, *talking about work*—that's work, too. But if you say The Big Guy won't mind, then I gotta go with that." Inside me, I laugh to an unspoken joke: how giving him guff like this *is* like a part-time job to me, and so that means I'm already working on a Sunday. He shakes his head so fast I almost think he didn't and then, when I catch up to him on his way to my shop, he shows me a real smile, and there he goes making me drop my guard again. He's talented. And on a separate note, I hope in about twenty years I look that good. Early fifties is what he's got going, by my estimate.

"The old catalpas, lindens by our church…the parsonage too…well, the wind'll snap off a limb sometimes."

"More often than here in the hollow, because they put your church on the highest spot in town…to be closer to You Know Who." I get nothing back, so I have to get serious. "Look, I'm no arborist. But how about I come up anyhow, bring down whatever's for sure dead?"

At this he stops walking and turns all the way towards me like something's going on. "I want you to fix my chain saw. The wife dropped me here on her way to visit one of our elderly who can't make it to services anymore. I rapped on your door, then I put the saw next to your shop. Kenny, I have to differ with you, about whose home is closer to The Lord. Do you understand? I walked the trail to your creek."

"Did Red get up with you?" I want to know. "The rooster, my one-bird welcoming party."

"No. Well, I didn't see him if he followed me."

"Water's high, isn't it?"

He ponders this longer than somebody who's just been to the creek should need to and then spills it out. "It's special Kenny. The sounds, the way the sunlight flashes around it, the whole experience there. Was your dad able to walk down there with you?"

I just tell him I've got my recollections and I lead him straight-line toward my shop, where I grab his saw on a swoop through the dark entry and hit the lights. *Let's get this figured out and give him the lowdown.*

This is so easy. *Why does something so easy have to take us to something awful?* "Aw, man, Rev. The piston's scored. That's why you can't pull the cord. And actually this means the whole thing's toast. I'm sorry, really."

But he isn't too shaken by this news and he even says, "So, there's no…*resurrecting* it?" And in this moment, for the first time ever, it's like we're two regular people, equal, neither of us with an agenda or a bone to pick. I chuckle for the both of us and back away from the bench. He goes on. "I've always wanted to see this shop where you had a chance to work with your dad when he could, rest his soul." I nod and that's all I can do, but he keeps going. "What's it been, six months?"

I'm trying to figure out what's stronger: how much I miss Dad when I peer up and down these walls that kept us stocked up and sheltered, or how grateful I am to the people of Reverend Bob's church for the way they afterwards managed to get the fist I had inside my chest unclenched. I can only shrug.

"That's how long you've been coming to our Sundays. It was October."

I'm rubbing my chin, but that's not satisfying when there's no stubble. "Well, it's about like you and the missus," I tell him, "being able to work together." Just then, in a ridiculous coincidence that yanks even Reverend Bob's lids up, the gravel crackles outside. "And that's the Mrs. Reverend Bob right there?"

He nods, proud as a peacock, and a glow is painting up his face in blotchy stages. "I adore her, Kenny." He can't help but tell me. "My ride. My everything." He sees me nod.

I'm a different generation, okay, and he knows I've never married—not me, no sir—but I understand exactly what he means and if that's not something, how about that he knows I do? I won't tell him my dad talked to me this way once about my dear dead mom, shortly before he himself passed.

But this gentleman here whose chain I'm always pulling lets the amount of time it *would've taken me to tell him* pass before he says, "Guess I better get out there. Roosters'll make that city girl skittish."

A couple days later, Reverend Bob called to say he was grateful for me looking at his chain saw.

"For me pronouncing it dead?" I asked him. "Tell you what, if I see one come through here where the people don't want it but I can breathe some life into it, I'll fix you up with it. In the meantime, you'll hear me when I get up there, let's say once a week or so, taking care of your downed wood."

Before he let me go, he asked would I help a few other guys with a little project in the church. They were going to subdivide a big room in the basement, and would I do the electrical? Sure. Then he said, and I'm still scratching my head about where he got it, "Oh, and Kenny…Al's got a chance…to keep that young family together, the little one and the wife."

I sucked air. "Yes." I wouldn't be tying one on with Al down at the Wooly Tongue again anytime soon.

He must have figured he got to me, guard down, because he called me again about a half hour later. "Kenny, you're someone I want to be able to talk to. I want to say what's on my mind sometimes and know that it's okay with you that I do."

Well, since he was on to something not up to something for a change, I told him I'm in, except for, "When you talk to me, do me a favor. What you believe, don't say it like it's a fact. That paints me into a corner. Just say *Here's what I think*. I mean, you can say it however you want from the pulpit. That's your house and if I'm out there, I'll think *OK*. But when it's just me, don't do that. Be real, already."

Wheels turned. "Deal."

I didn't want to be abrupt or anything, but I figured we were done, in a good way. "Bob, I for one think we're okay. Do you?"

The good man said yes, and we really were.

When the worship bell rang this time, I shot out of my seat and was second to the door, behind only Helen. No way was I going to let Erika corner me. Latex paint and varnish fumes rushed up my nose from those two new rooms down there. Upstairs in the sanctuary, I grabbed an aisle seat; first in, first out.

As the service begins, Reverend Bob says he's got an announcement and he hopes it's all right with everybody to do this before things get going. "Many of you are aware by now that we've converted our grade schoolers' room into two, one for the younger kids and one for the older. What you may not know is the sacrifice of the wonderful men who made this happen. I want to give you a chance to thank them right here." And with that, he throws both palms out and announces, "Bart, Joel, John Carrington, Kenny; won't you all come up here for just a minute?" The people start clapping, and Reverend Bob gets to waving us up. "I know each of you has a few words you'd like to share." Reverend Bob leaves the stage to the four of us.

Bart goes first. "So often it's hard to know what the Lord wants from us. It's a thrill when we actually know what it is." *Applause.*

John Carrington goes second. "Jesus said, basically, what you've done for the least of His people, you've done for Him, and that about sums up how I feel." *Applause.*

I'm fighting a grin over how he just inadvertently implied that the people in this congregation are the *least* of God's people, but then I realize they might try to make *me* talk.

Joel keeps the crowd on simmer. "Wherever two or three are gathered in His name, there is He also. And think, folks, we have an even better place to gather now." *Applause.*

It's obviously my turn, so I give just a sideways wave to the crowd, one that reminds me—and that's how stupid it is—of a wave Jim Carey might have made. Then I tap Joel on the back, like let's get the hell off the stage, and start to lead what I think is the procession down the steps and out of the spotlight. But Reverend Bob says, sing-songy, "Kenny, just a few words and accept our gratitude."

I fumble with my watch chain for what feels like a good ten seconds. Now I'm letting my mouth go, hoping like hell my thoughts catch up with it. "Well, I can think of a lot of projects where people aren't half so grateful." Nobody starts the clapping back up, so I add, "That's it," and mercifully they clap their hands raw as we make beelines back to our pews.

Sunday dinner is about the liveliest in my half a year. You'd think we were on drugs. Could be due to spring, which has certainly sprung. Helen has tears running down her cheeks, she's laughing so hard. If she pees in the booth, we might all get tossed, at least for a Sunday or two. We would then have to major suck up to Dick the owner because there's no place else in town to go. Helen has only started her story. It goes like this…she had opened the closet door and gone to put on her church jacket this morning, and there was Dwight, her cat (don't ask me) staring at it, like *Mom…*

"I've seen this once before, with one of Don's Carhartts," Helen says. "It's positively a mouse, but no telling which sleeve or pocket it's in."

"Well what, what'd you do?" Erika can't ever wait for anybody to do anything or say anything. It's not one of her many gifts.

"I got one of Don's contractor bags," and Helen's cracking up again, so none of us can be sure whether we're ever going to get to the end of this, but we really don't mind, "and I flicked the hanger off the rod so the whole coat dropped right into the bag. Then it's just a matter of squeezing the top closed and taking it outside."

Al's laughing. When his laugh fades, though, he asks politely, like if the story turns out to be a dud, he's going to thank Helen anyway for telling it, "But Helen, that's funny and all about Dwight, but then what?"

"Well then I get back in the house and Don says to me," and she's cracking up again, "Dwight just said *Did I ever take your TV clicker and throw it out in the flippin' yard?*"

The whole booth roars, so much that I think we may get the boot anyway if Dick happens to be in one of his frequent ugly moods. But he's not around, and I'm laughing an awfully good laugh, too, as if I didn't get made a fool of on the stage of that church across the street only a half hour ago.

Erika, in what somebody might not think is good taste, but I kind of do this time because she waited until all the laughing stopped, adds her two serious cents. "Wouldn't it be wonderful if Don would come to church with you, Helen? I mean the two of you seem to do so much together, and yet this one thing he apparently won't do for you."

Helen squirms and twists her shoulders back and forth.

Bart jumps in. "I wish I could get my wife to come. I can't. I can't."

Joel and his tiny wife are here with us for a change, and she has that *should I or shouldn't I* look, and throws her caution to the wind. "Well, I can't imagine not worshipping with Joel, or even worshipping someplace else besides with him." Joel squeezes her hand. All right, you can tell they're still in love. Good for them.

Helen, who's been sitting on my left, leans to my ear and whispers, "You do a little work for 'em or tell 'em an innocent story, and what do they do? Embarrass you."

Now I scramble to come up with something to fix this and I think *Here, this might do it, I don't know.* I say nice and loud for everybody to hear, "Hey Helen, you got that half acre woods on the side of your place. Maybe you see what I see? There's this little bit of time in the spring, two weeks, that's all, where the sun hits the ground cover and it shoots up. All the trillium and pasque flowers pop. Then, when the trees fill up, show's over. It all dies back to just a few inches off the ground. So if you miss it, you missed it."

"It's a sight, Kenny," Helen says. "You nailed it. This is when Don and I take our coffees outside, even if it's chilly."

She sweeps salt grains from the table and guides the shaker she's been fumbling with back to the center. "Those few minutes before he goes to work are so…romantic, I guess you could say."

Joel's wife parks her elbow, lays her finger along her bottom lip, and thinks out loud, "Oh, how lovely," and all around the booth, everyone nods. We're like a set of bobblehead dolls on a shaky card table, me included.

I'm up to my ass in lawn mowers and weed whackers, but I'm at the top of my game on this early Wednesday morning, repair-wise. All my diagnoses are dead nuts, and my tear-downs and put-back-togethers are perfect too. Time is money, as Einstein or whoever it was said, and making the most of your time is all about the sequence. But one thing is killing me today: paperwork. Not the fact that I have to do it; the fact that I'm not keeping the paperwork, especially parts prices, with the right job. I have a day like this once in a while, usually after I've been to the Wooly the night before, which is after all where I crawled in from last night. I need some life, is what it is. That son of a bitch Red woke me up and that's the only reason I'm in the shop early. I switch from radio to CD, rockabilly Jimmy Vaughn, and that helps only a little. But when the phone rings I get the improbable hope that she's cute on the other end, some damsel I haven't even had the imagination to see in my dreams, and that this conversation is going to make my day, if not my life.

It's Mister Clean, and he charges right into it. "Kenny, Bart. I can't talk. I need you to just listen and do what I say." He breathes out, flooding the mouthpiece with the sound a pervert would make. "Heather, my wife, she took lots of pills." I cut him off to ask how many and what kind, but he screams back, "An overdose. On purpose, all right? I need you to take whatever it is that's keeping you from the Lord, and get with Him this minute, and you pray for Heather, you hear me? Kenny, she might die!"

I have so many thoughts that they're in a logjam in my throat, where nothing out loud can come through.

Bart continues, "I know you don't claim to be saved. Just get with the Heavenly Father, and beg Him for my Heather's life! I gotta go."

I grab the boom box remote, accidentally press the volume-up and then the fast-forward button before the thumb I see shaking at the end of my hand finally finds the fucking OFF button.

My elbows drop to the bench. After a couple minutes, I flip somebody's job ticket over and draw an up-and-down line through the middle of it. Then I think better of this and take a fresh ticket to plot everything on. I title one side IF SHE LIVES and the other IF SHE DIES. That's the easy part. I scribble thoughts at the bottom, how these people are always talking about God's will; so if they always want God's will, what if it's God's will that she dies, and all of them are busy this minute begging God to do what He thinks is wrong?

I scratch all that out. I write, in big caps…

IF I WAS A PAGAN AND IT WAS <u>MY</u> WIFE
AND I ASKED YOU TO GET PAGAN SO YOU
CAN PRAY TO ALL MY PAGAN GODS TO
SAVE HER, WOULD <u>YOU</u> DO IT? YOU
ASSHOLES

I throw the pen across the shop to where I'll find it maybe next year and hope I never do, snatch the keys off the pegboard hook and walk out into a mist so thick the sleeves of·my jean jacket stick to my arms already before I get to the pickup. When the system injects that hurricane of air and fuel down into the caverns of the engine, the Big Old Pig starts with a roar and this gets me wondering, *Is Heather's heart roaring at this minute?* The Rs drop. I clunk into gear and the autopilot in me steers to the Wooly.

My boots on the boardwalk to the front door must have broadcast my arrival because, even before I pull it open, Goose has a brew poured for me. He barks "Cigarette!" and I flick it out the door. Never meant to bring it in. I drop onto a stool at the near end, not up in the middle like usual.

"Awful early," Goose says, and plunks the glass down in front of me, then shuffles off to do some mindless spill patrol. When he comes back, he's up for hobnob. "Talk about it?"

"Wife of a friend," is all I'm ready to let him know.

I've barely gotten it out before he throws me a warning. "Again? Kenny, what are you doing?"

I should've never brought Darla in here that one time. She's a walking list of I-shoulda-nevers, but the whole fling was my fault. Two-and-a-half months of tingle, but instead of your foot going to sleep, your whole mind did. It was like watching myself on TV, never knowing what was going to happen next and acting like it was somebody else's blockbuster story, and never having the simple good sense to shut that TV off. The year and a half since then seems like a lifetime, but obviously to only me. Now I can't have myself become talk of the town again.

"Goose, her name's Heather. I've never met her. She tried to kill herself and maybe did."

"Oh, like Buck's niece," Goose figures. "Trouble at home with this one, too?"

"Not that I'm aware. There's not much I know at all. Just...she was into that American Indian stuff, facing the four winds, shit like that."

Goose exhales through his nose and goes, "Christ. Well Kenny, this sounds like it's not your hand to play. It's gotta bring back memories of your dad, though, I'm sure. This is tough. Real tough."

I pour the beer down like my throat is a floor drain and slam the empty glass to the bar harder than I meant to, then offer "Oops" to sort of clarify things, that the Wooly's not for me just this instant.

Over the rise, the fog toys with lifting, and I can make out there's a clean white mommy van in the shop end of my driveway loop. It could be Reverend Bob, but he should be at the hospital, and I remember they've got just the one car between them, him and the missus. Red is hushed next to the door, so I'm dead sure I'm not getting ripped off. I did forget to flip my OPEN shingle around to CLOSED when I left in the huff, though, so this must be a *live one*. That's what I call customers when I'm talking to Red.

Inside the lights are on, but that's how I left the whole place. There's no sign of life and I'm thinking *Dad, help me here*, but in a second I hear the toilet flush and then the bathroom door creak open, accompanied by big-time sniffles. Around the tall and wide stack of cartons I call The Stink Wall comes Mindy, with eyes so pink they look diseased.

"Where's the boys?" I wonder out loud.

"With Jason. He stayed home from work. I told him I had to see the people from our Sunday group." She pauses to whimper. Now, I've known guys that get pissed off at this, but for me, it's always been a magnet that pulls me closer to the maiden in distress. It's how I'm constructed, and I think *Don't get me started on how, yes, my dad was too.* "I wasn't being nosey but I saw what you wrote, Kenny. On that paper." She sniffles. "I don't know how to talk to you."

"Then don't." This is gruff and all I mean is *Let it go*. So I have to grab this dear sweet thing's shoulder. Beats words.

"I feel so awwwful. First thing I thought of was your dad."

"Mindy, he was already very sick and he knew what he was doing." There's makeup fallout all over her bottom lids and her cheeks, so it looks like a pen exploded in her face. For the first time today, I think, true sadness grips me, and it's got a hell of a grip.

"I know," she says, and throws her arms around my neck.

A gush of Warm pours through me, a lot like the time I drank that radioactive shake to get my kidneys checked out. The hollow behind her ear has a scent I can only call precious. For the matter of a while, I understand that we *belong* together. Not like we'd make a great couple. All I mean is that, if a body lock like this one, so dreamy and complete and so chock-full of meaning ever happens in my life again, I'll know I don't deserve it. And I don't deserve to have it happen this time. Just as I manage to sum it all up to myself like this, Mindy rolls her head to my left and plants one burning wet kiss that lingers on my neck. This summons an undeniable rise from me, the first spontaneous in a good week. But I realize, as I walk her to her car in a minute, that I desire not one single other thing from Mindy, in her future or mine.

"I've prayed, Kenny. I've been praying nonstop since Bart called. But I can't share that with you, can I?"

"Let's go in."

Mindy takes a couple steps back toward the shop, so I bump and steer her onto the driveway toward the house. Her delicate crunches on the wet gravel suck my focus straight down to those slender ankles of hers. But I can say now and for all time, yes, they're out of this world, but they're not mine and I don't want them and they're more like priceless museum pieces anyway—everybody should have a chance to admire how beautiful they are and then everybody should go home to their own places and leave her be.

She's self-conscious about dragging the mud in, so I tell her it's okay to pop her shoes off, if she wants, and I head to the coffeemaker and vow to myself to not look whether she did. She follows me in her socks. "The whole thing is imposssssible," she says. "What's Bart supposed to do?"

"Look, Mindy, why do you think it's Bart's responsibility to do anything? I mean, he's beside himself, and he can't do *nothing at all*, so he does everything. He gets on the phone. Now everybody's supposed to do something. Everybody!"

"Kenny, you always say at Sunday School, *I don't have the same reference point the rest of you do and so don't let me hold you folks back.* Right? You say that. I know you mean it, but just once…can't you—"

"Can't I what, Mindy? Pretend?"

I'm not mad and she knows that, so if she wants to get to the bottom of this, let's go. But she goes quiet instead. She taps her long pink fingernails on the countertop maybe five times like a raccoon trying to open a walnut. The coffee's done, so I point to the living room. I know from church she likes it black, like I do, but there's honestly not that much else I know about Mindy.

The sweet thing is ready to get back to peeling the God onion. "You have *us* in your heart, but you won't let Him in."

I roll my eyes and I hear me huff, but I instantly feel the shame of this theatrical rudeness. So I think I owe it to her for me to explain. "God doesn't have your charm. You know, after the funeral, somebody called me every day." A lump is forming. "If it wasn't Al, it was Joel. If it wasn't Joel, it was Helen. Get it? *You* made a difference! It was like a tag team, and I'm sure you weren't even planning it together. Oh, you probably sometimes said, *I hope he's doing OK. Oh, yeah, he's starting to do better. I saw him Tuesday…*There were days when I'd get three calls. Least once a week, one of you would pull me out of here to grab a skillet or a sandwich or something at Dick's. See? I don't want to hear that crap about the devil and the loaves and the fishes—I want to hear your sweet voices. I don't want to recite those stupid verses—they sound like devil worshipper chants. I want to laugh with you guys. *You're* my addiction."

"But Kenny, our love comes from God."

"Well, I'm not gonna get into a goddamned argument with you about where *your* love comes from." This stormed out of me, starting that argument, stabbing our chat right in the heart and thoughtlessly sending poor Mindy—who managed to set her cup down without a sound—on a glide to her little shoes. I'm doing the only thing I can now, which is walk her all the way up the loop to her van. She runs the window down, and with a metallic slap of the bottom of her wedding ring against her driver door, pulls it closed between us. I ask her why she came. Really why.

"I realized when I got in the car this morning, you're the only one who lives where he works. So I knew I could find you. Well until I got here and you were gone. Kenny, I had to talk to *someone*. I can go home now. I can be ready for whatever. I'm just…" Mindy decides to not say more and puts it in gear. She turns the loop to the straight shot and of course, if there was a God, I'd be thanking him right now up and down for the fact that nothing happened between her and me. Nothing but the magic Warm I'm still thinking of.

I listen till the last crackle tells me she's not coming back to try and convert me or to cry some more. Then the breath goes out of me. I can't explain this, but I go to the spot where Ruffhouser used to lie by the heat register when he was really weak near the end, and then it hits me. When they die, I keep with me the moments when they were the weakest. Even though I had Ruffhouser from puppy, it still sticks in my mind what a wreck he became before the one morning when he was no more. I don't think of Mom that way because she went so quick, but Dad I keep in me walking crooked and not tall.

The register has a rust spot on it, from air conditioning condensate, shaped like California. After I got Ruffhouser diagnosed, I'd stare at that shape when one of us needed a break from me staring at him. A few of those times, I asked him would he fancy a trip to the Golden Gate Bridge.

I fetch the picture album off the mantle. Inside the back flap I have the few letters that a long time ago I put in date order, so on top is the one from when Dad wanted to come home.

Unredeemable

> *Kenny,*
>
> *Since you came out again for Kate's funeral I*
> *been thinking what if I move back. Your mom*
> *and me we got kind of snake bit here in Miles*
> *City, what with her heart and our troubles with*
> *the little herd and nobody decent to ride fence.*
> *The neighbors was always great I'll give em*
> *that. All the times they basicly took over things*
> *here when I couldn't get back from the hospital*
> *in Billings. I got no complaints about them. But*
> *it's lonesome anyhow. You and me Bud we*
> *always got along. Maybe I could help out in*
> *your shop. These bones is tired and I feel like*
> *crap a lot lately so it wouldn't be like full time*
> *or nothing. Not right off but think about it.*
> *One other thing Bud——I hope you shutted the*
> *damn door on that thing with Darla. Not a*
> *gentlemans way.*
> *Dad*

The day I got this, I called him the same night. The guy you could never get to say squat on the phone—he'd always say *Hang on* and give it to Mom, and then when she was done he'd grab it back and tell me *Make your old man proud now, that's it*—he all of a sudden yakked like a thirteen-year-old girl and gossiped about the patients in Mom's ward, the neighbors, who's on what side of the whole wolf issue, even about his neighbors' kids. I said he better get back home here and don't start watching Oprah in the meantime. When he said *g'bye*, he called me *Son*.

I slide the letter back under the flap. I know I won't be reading it again for a long time. I said my fitting and loving goodbyes, not just at his funeral but really every day at the shop before *and* after, and now I've got more sad in me? I grab my folder and my favorite pen from the nightstand, take those into the living room and sit down Indian-legged by the register, where I hear me say out loud, "Okay, Ruffhouser, help me out with this." I open up the folder to the only decent stationery I've got.

> *Dad,*
>
> *First-off I'm nothing but grateful to you. You don't know that yet. Grateful for telling me things you figured out so I wouldn't have to go and figure them out. For all the pictures you took when I was little. I look at those now and they always help me know who I am way on the inside. For not whupping on me when I grabbed the baseball bat and lopped the wood handle off that antique push mower in the shed—for how all you did was put your arm around me and say we're gonna come up with a way to not get so damn mad at stuff.*

I have to get away from it. I know what comes next, but not just now. I look up and dial Skinner Memorial. They go to a lot of trouble, ringing three stations before they track down Bart for me. And so for the second time in about ten minutes, I'm grateful enough to let whatever goodness is in me pour out, and there's a boatload.

Bart's pretty much spent, I can hear it. He talks soft, which isn't Bart. Heather's folks are around but they're in the cafeteria. He doesn't say a word about God or prayer, just tells me nobody knows anything yet and they won't know for a while. He *thanks* me for calling him. Thinking again about Dad's arm around me in the shed, I get a little dizzy. "Bart, I just started writing my dad a letter. Maybe you could write one, to Heather. Telling her things you know about her that she doesn't know you know. Things that drive you so nuts you don't know what to do with all that love."

Now *I'm* choking, *I'm* the one making the pervert noises into the phone. I apologize, but Bart says, "No no, Kenny. I never thought... See, everybody's scared to talk to me now, so of course they're not giving me any ideas what to do with myself here." I'm speechless, but Bart handles that, telling me there's construction in the lot by the river, so park on the other side of the wing if I come. "You're something, Kenny. This is what a *friend* does."

Back on the floor I whisper, "Ain't I a sight, Ruffhouser? Remind you of Shoshone Falls?" It's time to finish.

> The other thing is this. I forgive you. Some
> people said what a shame—that you had more
> living to do, and you know for a while I listened
> to them? But now I see it. I don't know what
> <u>finished</u> means as far as getting everything out
> of life but I sure know the things you did finish.
> Me for one. You got me to who I am, you and
> Mom both of course. Now I had a chance to tell
> her in Billings how I'd love her forever. That

was precious and I know you remember that. It's
high time I told you. I love you forever Daddy
and like you always said, That's one hell of a
long time.
Your Kenny

"Thanks, Ruffhouser." I give that fluffy ghost a thumb up, then fold the edges up all the way around the letter, strut to the truck and head toward the cape that runs out into the reservoir, the Belle Fourche. It's weird the whole way, not having the bass boat on the hitch, and I keep checking the rearview to see if it's wagging. I know Dad's not in the seat next to me, and it's not a Sunday morning, and we're not going fishing, but this so-familiar two-lane rolls its highlight reels anyway, one after another.

At the Fourche the breeze is wild, blowing ashes up out of the ash tray, and they swirl above the dashboard even though my window's down only a couple inches, so I tuck the letter into my Stetson and jam it on to where I usually don't if I care about hat hair that day.

My boots are clunking down the trail to the big water with the wind blowing tears and snot across my cheek, but guess what, I don't care and it even feels right. There's a red-tailed hawk very interested, or at least we're traveling companions. We both even hook left, to go along the bay that faces east, where it might be quiet enough to hear yourself think. I got a pretty spot in mind, but the waters are high with the snowmelt and spring rains, and there's all those lengths of shoreline where the slope runs all the way into the water, so not once, not twice, three times I plunk my whole right pasture boot into the bay. But the squish is just a souvenir and it doesn't annoy me. *See, Dad? We did come up with a way to not get so damn mad at stuff.*

And the spot is perfect. There's a pretty much rotted birch right above me. I can tell it's been thinking for months about falling over but it's still running its calculations. Just like Dad did till it was his time. The west wind has the flow headed straight out just like in my plan, so without another word to Dad or myself, I take the letter from my hat, rest it easy on the water of the bay, and watch until the flow delivers it intact into the body of the Fourche.

On the trail back to the Pig, the squish-clunk sets my hands to slapping out a rhythm on my thighs and chest. Soon this turns into Foosh-thud, clunk-slap. Foosh-thud, clunk-slap. It's a dance with no partner, but I have this flashing thought: who knows, I may just be finally fit, *worthy* Dad would call it, to take a woman into my life one of these days.

This morning Erika's motions remind me of Red on a mission, the way she's prancing around the classroom before Sunday School begins. I have to hit the coffee pot. As soon as I've poured a cup though, it dawns on me what a classic bad idea this is, given that I'm already pretty shaky from last night at the Wooly and that Styrofoam is such an ignorant invention—you can look at it wrong and it tips over.

When Sunday School begins, Erika opens. "Before we get started, let me turn it over to Bart for a few minutes. He's itching with news to share with all of us."

And Bart romps from somewhere in the back to get up there.

"I told Erika, I just wanna share with all of you…Heather came out of the hospital yesterday, and her prognosis is *no permanent damage*. I just have to say to all of you, because I know you prayed so hard for her, this is a testament of God's promise to listen to the faithful and hear their prayers. And now if I could…*Father, Your grace is infinite. You've heard the supplications of Your servants. We stand before You humble, ready to do Your…unending work. And we just ask that You just tell us what that is, as You always do, but we don't always seem to listen. In Jesus' name, Amen.* I'm so grateful to each and every one of you for praying so hard for my Heather." He's been looking down, stuck that way since his prayer, and he finally looks out at us. "And Kenny, I read her the letter." His mouth forms *Thank you*. Then, in about three seconds that remind me of the chief at the Hoffenbergs' barn fire, Bart presses to the door, where now he's off to the in-laws to fetch that wife he doesn't want to be away from, maybe anymore ever.

In the worship service that follows, Reverend Bob lays a similar announcement. "Many of you dream of greatness and aspire to it. But let me tell you, brothers and sisters, a great thing has been done in this church. One of our members has a loved one who was in grave physical danger and is now free of her affliction only because of the intercession of you good people with the loving Lord of Life."

On the steps after the service, Reverend Bob's all tied up with Doc Gray, so I figure I've got an easy escape to the diner. My first stride is a bit off, though. I'm always like that in bright light coming from someplace dark, and I slide a few inches on a pebble. This gives Erika a chance to grab my shirt cuff, blindside me. She's in that familiar Erika position already, wide base, like she's prepared to make an open-field tackle on me no matter which way I juke her, right here on the church apron. This'll be a question I guess, most likely a vague one. They call these *open* questions. I once read about this in one of their how-to-be-an-evangelist books when I was here changing a sink washer in the basement kitchen. A question like *Did the message this morning speak to you the way it did to me?* or maybe a dopey spray of good will, like *It's always nice to see you*, even though I haven't missed in seven or eight weeks, or—and I hope it's something like this—could I please pick up some certain somebody and bring them to Sunday School next week? 'Cause, yes I can.

She spins me a little towards her, and I find she's so nervous that her brows look almost angry. I'm affected for some reason, maybe church. I tuck my palm behind her triceps, just enough to touch that chiffon top she's got on, and I blurt out, "Go ahead, Erika. You really do have my attention."

She finds her fortitude or whatever and starts up, "When you weren't sure…Let me restart this…There you were, and Kenny, your father had lost consciousness and he wasn't ever going to regain it. Enough time has gone by now, I can ask you—"

But I don't have the heart to *not* cut her off. "Did I pray? Is that what you're wondering? No, Erika. I didn't buckle." She lets loose of my cuff and I hit the bricks, but then I pivot like a kid who realizes he's got only one of his gloves, and I bounce back up those few steps. By now, she's already got a young couple trapped in a new conversation, but I don't give a rip about interrupting. "Erika, the special today…Turkey and Stuffing, I think. Comin'?"

She nods and melts into the warmest smile I've seen from her in a month, and in case that wouldn't be clear enough, seals it with a pinky wave. Bart won't be at the diner with us today, of course. *I'll* be the one to defend Erika if she happens to stick her foot in her mouth. After all, I've still got that little bit of fixing to do.

Side Door

It was late February of 1975. My high school auditorium wasn't all that big unless you were, as I was on that Friday after my last class, alongside it and walking a U. First toward the face that fronted the visitor lot, next across the face, and then—with what I figured was going to be mounting dread—halfway toward the rear. Where I would stop walking and engage in this prearranged fight, by fists I suppose, though nobody had bothered to tell me about rules.

I turned that second corner, and because the walk pinched the building on its side, I had no angle yet to see up the stairs to the landing where Rick Stills, who was supposed to be my opponent, would be waiting.

For some reason, I had become impressed with the building, how homogenous the brick color, how manicured the shrubbery. *Parents, your kids go to a classy school, and don't you ever forget it.* This, I imagined, was the message in the meticulous care. As wet as it had been and on this shady side, there should have been some lichen on the barks as there always was at the preserve in town, but if there had been, it had all been killed. This painted another picture for me, one that was more comical but vivid, in which the administrators and groundskeepers wanted to kill all of us too, if they had a dark night and the right spray and something big enough to douse the entire student body.

But while I kept musing over the contempt the elders had for young shits like me, I was not entirely distracted from the revenge of a Rick Stills. Not calm exactly and certainly not arrogant or courageous. I was just wide open, inviting a sight or a sound to reveal why the hell I was even there.

This had all started on the Monday of that week, before Econ. Les slapped the back of my head, which was no call to arms because I was sure it was Les even before I turned around. He was always doing that.

"When did you piss off Rick Stills?" he asked me. "Now the guy wants a piece of you."

I didn't know anyone named Rick Stills, couldn't picture him, and had no idea whether we were talking about an adult or a fellow student. "What's a Rick Stills?"

Les pivoted on his heels and dropped his palm open to Carter, as if introducing a famous magician on some stage. Carter, as with Les, was also in my Econ class, so I thought nothing of the pirouette and expected nothing from Carter other than *Let's get in there already*. But Carter wrenched his pocked face into a contortion. He held up his Econ book about eye high, and pushing its spine toward me then pulling it back several times, used it like a pointing finger, but more threatening. "The guy hates you. So bad that there's a time and place."

With a flick of my forearm I shoved Carter's book right back at him and rolled my neck around to stare down Les, to get to the ha-ha that had to be coming. Now over Les's shoulder was The Wheeze, taller than us, looming and not giving away anything by eyes, by mouth, by word. For the first time, I got edgy—The Wheeze wasn't in our class, so I couldn't construct a reason why he was there.

"What do you have to say about this?" I asked him. I was trying to provoke something and I think I sounded pretty hostile.

"Stills's guys, *ek-hem*..." He used to clear his throat about ninety times a day. Too many soy harvests up that nose. "They came to us. They say you don't have a choice."

The bell rang, so Les and Carter and I blew into the classroom, and in under a minute, the world opened to micro facts, macro arguments. Good student as I was, I was no longer the focus of their nutty whim. I became a speck, a gnat riding on a wart on some horse's ass. But on this particular afternoon, for a change, I welcomed being that gnat.

When my last class was over I shuffled, with the amoeba-like mass, down the hall and peeled off at the library, where I pulled the yearbook to have a look at the photo of this guy Stills. There he was, someone I couldn't recall having met or seen. Next to his picture was the blank space where activities, if he had any, would have been listed. I tried to find some animosity in his eyes and couldn't. In fact there was nothing in his eyes. No edge, no curiosity, no dumb stare either. I got tired of trying to see something and flipped the pages to my own. There I was, a little naïve, a bit too hopeful looking, now that I studied my picture. In the activities space was Football So,Jr; Baseball Fr,So. *That's it?* Now I was somebody else trying to figure me out, then somebody bored who wanted to flip pages to find a more interesting person.

Tuesday was always The Wheeze's day to slop the hogs after school. We all knew this. His family was big, so this chore was considered small, but serious just the same. So I was almost startled when I popped the school's heavy front door open and saw him at the bottom of the wide concrete steps, next to Carter, next to Les.

And next to Les was Piper, whom I'd hardly seen since freshman Bio. Wheeze pointed at Piper. "She knows one of Stills's guys. McClow."

"So what?" I said to Wheeze, I guess to Piper too.

"Please be very careful," she said.

"Careful about what?" I wanted to hit Les and shove Carter and tell Wheeze to go home and shake my head at Piper, just didn't know which to do first, but soon details were flying. Not a lot of details, only *Friday, 4:45, far side door of the auditorium.*

"This way," Carter said, "they figure everybody'll be cleared out."

Yeah, maybe me too, I thought.

On the approach to the steps up to the alcove where I would find Stills, I got a hot flash that reminded me of one time Les and I went up to Canada to ski. They had a race course set and we paid our money to get registered without thinking much about it. Then when I got to the starting position, I felt I should have thought about it. Instead of your shins pushing out a wand to start the timer yourself, two horse gates fly open to start it. But before they do, you stare ahead at nothing but the two hinged gates, as if they're an opposite wall in a room you can't get out of. You don't know exactly when they'll open. All you know is that, if you crash them before they do, you're DQ-ed for that run, and if you do that twice, you're DQ-ed for the race. I false started my first run. On my second, when the gates did open, I had a sickening feeling that I'd been staring through those now-open gates, not moving, not reacting, for a ridiculous amount of time. The hot flash.

So there I was, with the stairs in view and a blast of hot air in me, thinking, *How long have I been staring at* this *mess? How long have I been accepting that I had to come here, that I had to fight?* Too late to start thinking.

Just a few minutes earlier, when I was trudging the walk on the other—the bright—side of the auditorium, I remembered how my older sister Donna's voice had resonated so purely on the other side of the vast brick wall and filled the great hall for all the parents. The madrigals were otherworldly but she, for her part, was angelic. Her notes were dipping and diving and soaring back up to that ornate ceiling. She took Dad's breath away. I watched him. He couldn't muster so much as a whisper to Mom. Afterward, we all followed his hush to the visitor lot where, when it was time to unlock the car, he stopped. He said just, "That was somethin'."

I remembered my brother's Willy Loman in *Death of a Salesman*, how he pulled everyone into himself, that the audience had clung to his every word. Now he too had gone off to college where he was nailing his engineering courses and doing his own laundry so that, when he came home, he wasn't dumping anything on Mom. The night of the play, Mom glowed that glow I recognized from her wedding picture. She had been showing the world there shouldn't be any question, not about Dad's getting furloughed every few years and certainly not about the precious little successes she knew would spawn within those ugly pea-green walls of the bungalow she was then about to move into.

My stroll to the side door had been mechanical. Mindless, I could see that. What I had recalled of my sister's and brother's accomplishments had been trying to tell me something, that I might ruin this sanctified place for my parents, for ever. *What was it that I didn't understand before I turned the corner from the* proud *face of that building?*

I got a few steps from the top when I looked around, all the way around, and made an observation so cocksure that it blurted right out as if I were deliberately offering Stills a conversation starter to do with as he pleased. "What's this? You've got a coat on. I've got a coat on. And none of our coat holders are anywhere in sight." Then, with no control or forethought, I laughed, and stepped up to the deck of the alcove.

The guy took a single step toward me, not laughing. Not insulted looking, though. Not anything, just like in the yearbook. But finally I could size him up. He had probably an inch on me in height, but shorter arms. I may have had a reach advantage. I gave him a good fifteen pounds more weight, too, but I didn't think that should be a problem. *Can't read attitude and don't know his skills or experience at this, but things should be pretty even*, I thought. Then I remembered I had no experience at this.

No one had ever said I was the combative type. In football camp, when the coaches were somewhere else timing sprints or bitching at a player for eating too many salt tablets, I was the one who was breaking up the little fights. I never took sides, so how could I ever have made an enemy? I was mulling all this, turning my back to Stills, until I woke back into the present at the sound of his crepe soles whisking toward me.

"You're too trusting," he said.

"Maybe. Maybe I think…if you're really mad at me, you should be ranting about whatever it is."

"*I'm* mad at *you?*"

Oh, geez. He was serious. For a second time I laughed, for a second time he didn't.

"Griff," I said, and held out my hand for shaking.

He met it. "Rick." Then he dropped my hand as if a timer had expired or it was too chummy for what he wanted to say next. "What did you need them for anyway?"

How to do this without insulting the guy's intelligence was what I didn't know, but as with all my other casual behaviors that day, I flicked the dilemma to the wind. "We're the brunt of their big joke. I'm a brunt. You're a brunt, Rick."

Now one end of his wide mouth curled up, threatened to smirk, which he didn't. But he did understand, at last. He made a pooh puff through his lips, one that must have been blocking him from talking, and now the dam had broken. You couldn't have gotten him to shut up, not by interrupting, not by making faces. I know, I tried. Most of it was how your friends don't know what you really want, how they try to do your thinking for you. Midway he coughed a little, like The Wheeze, then blurted out, "I gotta not do that. I got testicular cancer." Before I could say I'm sorry, though, he pushed right back into all the things he felt like telling me, some from logic, some from stream of consciousness.

Okay, I thought, *I was feeling bad about not knowing how or when to say I'm sorry about his sickness, and now I'm feeling bad about wanting to walk away.*

That's when Stills cut loose an idea. "We ought to get 'em back for this."

I was enrolled. We would tell them they needed to be present and that, when they were, it would be all the fight they were hoping for. Of course we wouldn't fight. We would shame them, then walk away. We set it for the following Friday, 4:45. Side door.

Déjà vu. I had turned that final corner of the U and was heading back toward the steps. This time I was chuckling about my student body spray thought from a week ago, about how this all turned out, especially about what we were going to do to our friends. I hoped they didn't see how light my stride was, but wait, it didn't matter if they saw me laughing. They could take that to mean I was just confident, smug that I was going to reduce this Stills guy to regretful.

The Wheeze was there with my group, walking toward me from where the sidewalk met the steps. He was clearing his throat, which I took to mean that he was nervous about what he wanted to say, but that it would be this: I shouldn't go through with the fight. When I reached them, they were all silent. Carter wouldn't look at me. Les looked like he was about to put a puppy to sleep.

Stills' guys sounded like they were arguing with each other. There were only two of them. Their tiff wasn't heavy, but it was some difference of opinion I couldn't hear well enough to distinguish.

According to our script, when I reached the bottom of the steps to the alcove, Rick at the top and I down there each shed our coats. I handed mine to Les. Rick tossed his to one of his buddies.

I reached the top and said to Rick right away, "I hope you're ready for this." Real loud, taunting.

He said, "I can't wait," and he laughed, actually laughed.

We both turned now to face the instigators below and said, in church-like unison, "You ignorant shits!" Then he and I shook hands.

His guys headed to the visitor lot with some fire in their asses. Les and Carter took to whispering to each other, then followed them. The Wheeze was looking up at me, but he couldn't stop coughing, so I was going to accept that as an apology. I cupped my palm on Rick's shoulder like, *Good job, Bud.* At this, The Wheeze double-timed to catch up with Les and Carter.

I made the flight down to where they had dropped the coats and tossed Rick's up to him, though he was halfway down himself already. He put his on. I put mine on and waved *See ya* back at him.

But I thought better about just flat leaving. I wished I had a couple Budweisers stashed in the bushes for us. "Hey Rick. I got my motorcycle today. Hop on? Get some pizza? I'm thinkin'…Al's Big Pan."

"You go."

"I know, their sausage tastes like bologna. But there's an old guy there I can maybe get to bring us out a couple Buds.

Wouldn't be the first time. What a story that would make when our guys find out—you and me?"

Rick was lumbering toward the auxiliary lot in back. As if he didn't hear, but he did.

I had thought I might do one good thing myself on the dark side of this stupid sanctified hall. "No?" I hollered.

And that stopped him, his dark coat swiveled. "You don't listen," he said. He spun around on his toes, came back to me and squared, face to face. Hauled off a fast upper cut that stopped when it barely thudded against my gut. "I told you I was sick." This time he really did walk away.

I *didn't have* Dad's old Indian. Why did I think I rode that machine on that day? I just wanted to wake up tomorrow and be me, take a long ride, blow that place off of me. If I would catch myself forgetting to appreciate the sweet rush of the wind against my face because, out of the blue, I would envision myself in a tie and jacket somewhere, interpreting a market downturn or predicting upward pressure on commodities, that might feel just right. The rest of it could wait till Monday or keep waiting, for all I cared. Saturday could become my new favorite day of the week, like Mom and Dad with their Thursday date nights—you didn't get in their way. A breakout, then rinse and repeat. The young punk on the tired old Indian.

These days the sport coat *is* my uniform when I'm on TV or a vlog as the special long-in-the-tooth academia nut. I always caveat my economic forecast with my degree of confidence, since this still is a mysterious and dangerous world. We call the factors moving parts because they do move.

Observe, observe, observe, I urge the viewers. Listen. But don't trust. One Richard Stills would be proud, if he's among the living.

The Purpose of Sunday Afternoon

Dad picks up another birthday card from the coffee table, and it flaps a little as his hand vibrates. The once sinewy and steady hand has been evolving into a hock with gnarls. This gets me considering my own.

Oh yeah, the card...I know the senders. This spares me hearing who they are, who their children are, and their children's children. I'm tightening my temperamental B string to pitch, glancing to the unforgiving clock, nodding toward the card. We have songs to make perfect and only one other practice before our gig.

The hand sifts through what I call *the debris* on the coffee table. There must be another card that's critical for me to hear. I don't read them, I listen to Dad enunciate their sentiments. I'm crazy about Dad's voice. He's so crazy about it that he sings in public places, even restrooms.

I'm tuned up. We'll take it from the top, but first he'll offer me hard candy, then leftovers in flap-seal baggies from the fridge, mostly dinner rolls he was served in the big fancy dining room downstairs. There's nothing paltry about these. They're all treasures to him.

He moves fast from the kitchen, weaving around the piano he doesn't play, the rocker he doesn't sit in, and the guitar case he doesn't expect in his way and knocks over.

The excitement begins, not with the collision, but with the attempt to catch the case on its way down. I'm scared, and tickled by his bumbling good intentions, but I don't want to get so used to being tickled that I lose my fear about him.

It's beach weather in his apartment, and one of us is dressed right. He's in his requisite running shorts and a clashing T-shirt from a 5K. His feet bare but for sandals. I drove an hour on snowy roads, had to shed my own shirt right away, and continue to slow roast.

I wanted to mention something about the first song, but the sight of those leg veins, how dark a blue, must've choked the big idea right out of me. And a waft of his freshly cut toenails, well…I'm sure I'm not making a face, but he puffs through those wide nostrils anyway, and his familiar simper broadens till it opens to frame the tooth he cracked on pavement in a 5K just last August.

Oh, it was the timing, that he doesn't need to give each beat an identical vocal time cycle. *Syncopate this thing a little, for cryin' out loud.* He moves to the couch, next to me. Good, he'll be able to hear better.

A cloud has opened up, so the sun gushes in to bathe the dated love seat parked in what should be the swift exit path to his apartment door. Someday I'll recommend a different layout, maybe draw it on paper first. Or did I already do that after Mom died, when it felt so important to pack out the pain in boxes?

I strike up the intro.

"I'm an old cowhand…from the Rio Grande" soars from his throat, booms off the far wall, and floods the room with melody.

Good, Dad. That was just right. Better than right.

Rori's Words

"Rori honey, sit down," Daniel admonishes his eight-year old daughter, as if we're in church and a sermon is about to be delivered. Sit down? Why doesn't she loll over to the counter and ask the woman in the flowered print smock, *Is it okay to take one of those candies from the dish*? Or why doesn't she go and whisper *Pretty Boy* into the parrot's cage if she wants to, or stroke the tabby's head? Here's a better one: why don't the two of us grown men just sit here with Radar between us and shut up. But I've got a good ten years on Daniel and I don't want to sound condescending, so I bite my tongue.

Radar is some kind of terrier mix, about twenty pounds of bristle and the good nature they've told me about. We're here to get the wonder put back into him. This whole time, he hasn't even been curious about the odd and random population of this waiting room. I'd be happy if he'd just reach down from the bench, do a soft landing, and take a leak. Anything. But his eyes are foggy. He'll look at me when I rest my fingertips on that wooly hair behind his ears, but he won't *really* look at me. He won't really look at Daniel or Rori, for that matter, and that's all I've wanted to see for the last hour.

Daniel keeps pushing one foot out, then the other, about every half minute in a sad cross between a seated Hokey Pokey and an unconscious loafers and argyles fashion show. This is almost in sync with what he's got going with his hands. First they're in a clasp between his thighs, then they're fisted and jammed into his windbreaker pockets.

"Did you call Rori's mom?" I'm probing. My own ears tell me right away this is snoopy, but it might help us with the waiting if he would talk.

"I had Rori's grandma on the phone coming up the hill," Daniel says. "Trouble is, she's got no way to get here from Bull Shoals even if Radar doesn't pull through. Best way she could help now, like I told her, start calling Rori every day or so, you know, for a while…Hey, you managed this hill pretty decent on that bicycle."

"That's why they make those low-low gears." Now I see that asking about the kid's mom was intrusive. I'll let that rest and concede that fidgeting *may be* the best thing we can do right now.

Eight-by-ten glossies of purebreds in a garish arrangement take up most of the real estate on the big wall. I guess you could bring your Shepherd here and point at the Shepherd on the wall and tell yourself that yours sees theirs and gets it. But today this wall is a mockery, all these perfect dogs in their glam shots presiding over the lobby where real dogs like Radar lie broken.

At least Brenda will fix him. Or she'll know what to do.

Of course I haven't seen her since Dart, my Himalayan, died a couple years ago. It was when he finally stopped eating, after two-and-a-half years of me forcing pills and shooting liquids down his throat, seven times a day. Dart was saying, *That'll be that.*

I had saved him from an abusive couple, neighbors of a union buddy who got tired of listening to the jerks scream at their kitten. They handed Dart to me with a rubber band around his neck. *Here.* I had just offered to take him away if they really didn't like him, and for the next thirteen years he made me laugh, every day. He turned me—the notorious dog guy—into a bona fide Cat Appreciator.

The second day I had him, my sister deposited my little niece at the house to check him out. When she was petting him, she absentmindedly shared a little secret. "Mom says it's weird you have a kitten."

I said, "Oh, yeah?" poking, the way I do with as few words as possible, and Cara took the bait.

"She says because you're tough as nails, it's gotta *look* silly. But I don't think so." I gave her the eyebrows up. "She says you need something you can run with. Throw a ball to." Then Cara sighed, like she just solved a hard puzzle, and immediately got too amused with the new kitten to go on with whatever else my gossipy sister had been saying.

"Hey, he's gonna be your auntie's cat as much as mine. We made this decision together." We were supposed to, so I guess this was close enough to true. "Now let me show you a cool trick he does."

She said, "I know what it is. He rolls over and lets me rub his belly."

"No, Sweetie. I mean that's a good one, too, but that's not it. He hides! Watch him. Watch him hide and then dart out and scare his mouse." I grabbed the toy fishing pole, counted down for the kitten "Ready…set," and he backed up behind the recliner, like he'd been doing for me, just enough where neither of us could see him. I counted off a few seconds, flicked the pole so his mouse on the line landed right next to the chair. And on this cue, Dart shot out from behind the chair, pounced his two front feet smack onto that mouse, and then stood back and looked up at his new dad and new cousin, with *How'd I do?* written all over that pushed-in face.

That's when Cara said, "Uncle Jimmy. You got to call him Dart."

When he dropped to five pounds, less than half his normal weight, I was here with him every other day, six times in those last two weeks. The visit before the last, Brenda told me, "Jimmy, he's not suffering." That there was no pain. She went over how a cat in pain'll do almost anything to make it not show—calling on instinct or some such—but insisted that was not what was happening to Dart. "Trust me. This little guy's thinking, *Dad's here, so life is good.*"

"He's listing to the right," I argued back, "and twice yesterday, he listed so bad he fell over."

She would have none of it. She repeated herself. "Life's good because his dad is here." But on that, she went utterly quiet. This tower of animal hospital strength, who's always got yarns to spin and options to roll out, went mum. When she spoke again, she said, "Of course, there's nowhere to head next. Surgery's out…and there is something to be said for being able to choose. I mean, you and I won't be able to do that for ourselves."

I gave her one sharp nod, guided Dart into his travel case and pulled the door. But damn if Brenda didn't punch me square in the shoulder blade. It turned out, she wasn't finished.

"Jimmy. I'm trying to get you a few more days with Dart, is all. And you know why."

My wife had left three weeks earlier, planting the kiss of death on our wounded and childless marriage. Brenda's not a family friend, but I had let this much out in the first of the recent visits. She had always known me with my wife so she was curious. It's her job to be curious, too, I eventually figured, since you would never want to see one spouse make a major pet decision to spite the other.

Splitsville, Disappear-o, that's all I'd said about where my wife had gone and the prospect of her coming back. That's all I had known. "Brenda, I won't keep Dart alive like this just to make *me* feel better," I said.

But I saw that this got her digging. It was the look people have when they're thinking to themselves, *Okay, be careful how you couch the next thing*. Out of respect for Brenda, I wasn't going to let her pull our exchange down to complicated and pointless apologies, so I fixed my eyes on hers and used a kind of Peter Jennings tone to deliver my inalterable fact in a blanket of empathy. "Look. No one could've done better by Dart than you and I have…and soon we'll do the one last good thing." And I walked away as fast as I could, so she wouldn't think I was hoping she would say more.

Now, if you've really got to usher a creature you adore across that Rainbow Bridge that every mature pet owner has heard of and dreads, you'll need a Brenda to do the ushering. She took care of Dart, of me, whispered to *both* of us, laid a couple fingers on Dart's paw and then on my wrist, and then went away, and I know she would've let me stay in that special goodbye room all day with Dart if I wanted to.

She had to make sure everything went right. When she folded up the stethoscope to stick in her pocket, the click of those stems sounded like the boots of a soldier coming to attention for a final show of respect. And she asked me, "Can I have a hug?" My body had no mass, as if I'd been fasting without sleep for days. It stunned me how easy it was to lay my lifeless Dart on the chair and stand up. Brenda's arms, hefty like they are, formed a circle I was suddenly and entirely within, and this hug was none of that tap-tap crap. Everything *was not* going to be okay—the hole in my life had just gone from big to huge—and she didn't try saying that things would be, but a teardrop fell from her cheek and landed on my left hand when we broke the embrace. She whisked out the door with the grace of a sheet of paper blowing off a desk. I turned back around with a mighty certainty for the next thing to do and smeared her tear onto Dart's face. Then I lifted his little body and held him against my neck for who knows how long, but a perfect amount of time.

God, Brenda, where are you? Daniel's silence is driving me stir-crazy, and my butt bones have had it with this oak bench. I get up quietly, drift to the window. How many times I've stared out of it, too many, poring over our little east-central Missouri village. From here, its buildings look like matchboxes and the people look like map pins, but today the view is wildly different. It's Oktoberfest here in little Germany. One day of the year you'll see this. Down the hill by the rail tracks, between the rows of red brick storefronts that line Ribbon Street, semi trailers are parked, and their cargo is sprawled like muddy boots dropped on either side of a corridor kitchen floor. And all of this chaos here in Dittersdorf is, in fact, how I wound up at the vet.

From my house on the opposite hill, the other side of town, I was headed down for the fair this morning. Flying, more like it, on my old twelve-speed. And I prefer the bike to the big van for this because I don't have to park a half mile away and it's easy to leave when I feel like it. The two downtown blocks were clogged with pedestrians reading festival leaflets and losing their battles to keep their kids at their sides.

I was doing maybe 15, pretty fast. Something shot out from between the parked cars on my right, I heard a yelp and I was airborne over the handlebars. I remember scrambling to get my bike out of the middle of Ribbon Street because cars were everywhere. An old woman rolled her window down and asked me, "Are you all right, dear?" I dragged the bike to the curb. My ball cap was still on the street and nobody had run over it, so I retrieved that.

On the sidewalk, an old man with lures in his hat said, "Wow." A gorgeous blonde grabbed my forearm and said, "What…on…earth?" and my friend Dusty who played second opposite me at short on an unfortunate fast-pitch team four years ago ran toward me, yelled "Safe!" and watched, as I did, a hunk of hot dog bun shoot out of his mouth. "I saw the whole thing. I think you've got a good case!" A glance to the pavement told me cars were still stopped, but no drivers were antsy.

The most precious little girl I think I've ever seen crossed the street toward me and she said in a spooky monotone, "Mister. You hurt my dog."

Her eyes were wet underneath her brown curls. I was still swooning from getting upended and I opened my mouth, but no words came out. In that moment I thought I had to know more, but I didn't know what it was I had to know. Maybe this is what hypnotized feels like. The little angel in her baby-blue hoody and pink tennies was struggling to hold a ball of fur. Only then did I realize I was supposed to be paying attention to her dog. All I wanted to do was kneel and look at her dog, but for some reason, I was standing there the way I would if I were waiting for someone ahead of me to move along at a salad bar.

Then came a man, thirty-ish, in business casuals. "Rori, keep moving," he said. "Up on the sidewalk." He took the white dog from the girl how a mother might receive her newborn from the obstetrician, then squinted at me and asked whether I wanted to call someone. About my elbows and knees, I guess.

With a bravura that startled even me, I snapped out my right arm to point. "See that tan building up the hill? Let's go there *now*. I'll be right behind you."

The score inside here is Animal Smells 16, Disinfectants 7, and I can't make my nose stop keeping track. Daniel has finally got Rori convinced that she's the only one who can comfort Radar so, now free, he gets himself to the window to stand by me.

"I appreciate you still being here," he starts. "It's got to be helping her to see that you care too. You know, those two used to be inseparable, her and Radar. Grew up together, basically. Everything changed when her mom walked out in March. School." A chuckle bursts out of the good little man. "It used to be like a game Rori played with us, yack yack yack about all the things she was learning. You couldn't get a word in edgewise at the dinner table. Her mom and I would wink to each other and let Rori go ahead and spill it all out. We'd lay awake later giggling about how fascinated Rori was."

Daniel pauses, so I step in just to get him to start up again. "That fits. I mean, with how serious she is for eight. Focused. Yeah."

"Oh, she's serious, alright, but I can't say focused. She's slipping, Jim. She's slipping into…just preferring to be alone. Her *words* are gone, like somebody stole them."

Now he turns to face the window and closes the door on what happened to their marriage, on what anyone can do to give Rori hope, on why this child didn't latch onto her dog all the harder since her mom left.

Don't be a jerk and go and tell your story, I think to myself. *That would be comparing. This is entirely about the little girl.* "In due time, Daniel," I tell him, and I can see he's done. Tired done.

A skinny little redhead in one of those smocks stands with her foot propping the hallway door open and breaks our latest silent streak as she calls out, "Radar?"

Mechanically we move, but we're listening as we do. Doors are slamming and pets are shrieking in terror. All three of us wince. Maybe Radar also does, though he's being carried. I wish I were being carried. No, having my hand held. *Too familiar*, but there's nothing to say about my times here that could help Rori or Daniel in any way.

Finally Brenda makes two taps on our examining room door. The first thing she does is pat Rori's head and say sweetly to her, "Hi, Cutie." Brenda throws a glance to my face and then to her own feet, where it lingers, so I fold my arms across my chest like this stance of mine will ward off bad news, if there is any. But she opens her mouth a good few seconds before speaking, "Those diagnostics we did when you came in…They don't look so good."

With no thought or plan, I find myself slaloming to the left around Daniel and then to the right around Brenda. I yank the heavy door and I bolt for the lobby and beyond, where I get as far as their dwarf red bushes before I get sick.

My palms are stuck to the knees of my jeans. But with every drum beat of my heart on the wall of my chest, I'm able to loosen my fingers a little. It's then I remember to breathe. A small voice, unambiguous like your conscience in a movie, tells me, *Go back in*. I'm grateful the voice waited till I had my breath, so I waddle up the walkway, and the steps too, all the way to the door. My hand slides right off that handle though, because in the shiny glass is one of those scream caricatures, wearing my black T-shirt and my Royals hat.

Two weeks later on a Friday, Dusty came by. I saw that ratty pickup turn into my driveway. I remember flinching a lot, as if I were getting small electrical shocks every time there was a noise, and there were plenty——the squeak of his brakes, the boom of his door shutting against apparently no weatherstripping, and the fizzes of two beers opening. We plopped our butts down on my picnic table in the front yard. Between my invincible white pine and the overgrown juniper is a look at downtown Dittersdorf that you would get in the viewfinder of a camera turned vertical. It was dusk. I realized right away that I had been needing some of this softness around the edges of things.

"So, you didn't have to have stitches or anything?" Dusty said.

I heard me let out a laugh. We went on to cover a few more things, the tournament where we actually did play very good ball. We remembered getting a lot of runners *on* that year and how we just weren't knocking 'em in with any consistency. He told me Curt our left fielder was moving to Arizona in a week, which was news to me.

When I walked him back to his clunker, Dusty held his door open and backed out. I remembered he always did that at the ball yard after games. I guess he hates mirrors. Door still open, he rolled back up to me. He said he had to know, "What ever happened to that dog?" I just said I never found out. Fact is, I hadn't thought Dusty was aware of anything that took place after he'd made light of things and pissed me off down there in town.

This morning has turned out crisp and blue. I jumped into the van and went to see Brenda, where somehow, without trying very hard, I managed to finagle Daniel's address out of her. She was busy, and neither of us said boo about what may have become of Radar.

I traversed that hill, parked in front of their house. Guts I've got. I spotted Rori in the big front yard tossing a ball over her head and catching it in her tiny glove, so I grabbed mine from under the seat.

Easy. Do everything easy. I ease my knee onto the grass next to her. My jeans are sticking to the scabs, so I have to suck it up just to choke out, "Hi ya, beautiful." She's peering at me with her head kind of tilted, that's all. So I say, "You know me, right?"

She leans to my ear, whispers, "You ran over Radar."

Her eyes are dark brown. Her teeth are short, and it strikes me this is the only distinction between Rori here and the movie star she could someday be.

"I know y'all're mad at me." One of her laces has come loose and is lying across the blades of grass. "Mind if I tie this for you?"

"Nope," she says, puffy on the P.

I snug her pink tennie up and give it two sharp *there-you-go* slaps. And I offer up, "Let me toss you a couple."

She treads backward to what seems a very right distance to play catch.

"You got an arm on you," I say, but with so much enthusiasm it sounds forced and dishonest. So she does the duckbill thing with her lips that I saw her do when Daniel told her to sit down at the vet's. "You go to Truman, don't you?" I don't expect a response. And I don't get one. "Well, I think it looks like a nice school. So! Do you like it?"

At this Rori droops, could be deliberating. Words might come next, I think, but I'm wrong.

"Rori…when do you get to see your mom?"

She zings the throw back. Returns three or four more. Now she holds the ball out to her side, sunny-side up, the way you might absentmindedly hold the next apple for a horse behind you. "Every night," she says. "Almost every."

I peel off my glove, hold it in my throwing hand. Daniel told me his ex now lives in Kansas City. That's three hours.

"In the kitchen…Daddy holds her hands. He looks at her."

Still baffled and hating that I am, I say, "I kinda meant the times when *you* get to talk to her." Rori shakes her head in slow-mo and I already regret interrupting her. Six years as president for the manufacturing union local at the plant has puffed me up with a lofty sense of conversational mission, as if it's my job to keep everybody on the subject at hand. I always want to be careful to not sound like I'm steering. Marriage gave me a ton of practice at reining it in but I'm sure I still—in the delicate parlance of my ex-wife—*generally suck at it.*

"Guess you wouldn't feel right horning in on their time together?" I ask her, to pry Rori's voice back open if I just can.

She kicks a leaf on the grass. She shakes her head very fast this time, with a little tip to it that signals me I missed something. "I'm sleeeeping," she says, and I feel me bite my lip, and the machine that was cranking out all these questions screeches and halts, the way The Monsters at the plant do at the end of the second shift.

Rori does throw the ball back, and I'm grateful. Grateful to a child, because now we can retreat to the expected back and forth, the language we both understand. But now I toss one too high and she's got to chase it. As she bends to pick it up, Radar lumbers into my field of vision from I suppose somewhere uphill around the house. He snatches up the ball and takes a few paces in reverse with his tail fanning, like, *Want yer ball? Come 'n' get it.*

Daniel is standing at the corner of the garage with the business end of a leash at his left hip and his right arm raised from the elbow, palm out, in a stance fit for taking the oath of office. So I return the good man's salute.

Back in the van, I push the window lever down to flick out a bur oak leaf that's stuck in the web of my glove. But now I leave it there and slide the glove under my driver's seat.

When the first week of April comes around next year, the scent of damp grass will funnel up my nose, and the sounds I conjure to myself—like the thwack of a bat against a ball—will begin to slice up like crocuses through that overwinter crust blanketing the restless ballplayer in me. I will breathe. I operate this subterranean factory in my mind, where I stamp out vignettes of double plays and game-winning singles for the season we're about to start.

I'll reach under the seat, pull up my glove, and this leathery leaf will still be there. This is what I like about these. Time passes. Sure. And their heyday may be over, but they're damn tough and they're not going anywhere. They stick around.

Whose Will Be What

A guy I call Chef has asked me, can he have my socks? He made something like fatback for our dinner. And string beans from a can—I know I'm right about that part. We're in The Chef's car. Other times we eat in mine, I think, or each in our own. I can't make it to mine tonight, so I have to ask him to go and get that padded thing I sleep in, but I can't remember what it's called. I *need* it. I'm so cold.

I hear me groaning, feel me shivering. But I'm not sitting in a car after all, I'm lying flat on something. It's not dark like I thought, it's very bright. Eyes flutter. Now they're open, and something floods into me and it's not bad, it's pleasant. It's not narrow like that dream or cropped like a photo, it's wide like everything everywhere. That's right…it's my surgery day. It must be over. I'm sure it is. But I'm so cold.

She's laying a heavy blanket over me, the nurse, and it is toasty. She moves around in starchy jerks, and I believe I heard her cluck when I'd first tried to speak. Severely official is how I sum this up, credentialed in some nonspecific indignation. When she says the word *soon*, she says it the way someone would say *At 4:09*. Soon they'll make me sit up and drink juice, and soon after that the doctor will explain things. And my hired ride guy is waiting. The thing about hospitals is they take really good care of themselves, snip away any notion of suing them a patient may sprout, before that notion can grow to a mass. They won't do an operation or let you go home unless you have someone. Someone to drive you…

Someone to nod when they go over your new pills to stop and get, and to nod with even more enthusiasm when they say to call their hotline if anything seems weird. Come on. They know *everything's* going to seem weird.

The pain, the bandages, sponge-bathing. These the doctor goes over first. He's got an unsightly mole next to the corner of his mouth. Makes him look shifty. That's what I thought the first time I saw it and that's what I think again now. Maybe he is shifty. I want to tell him he should get it looked at.

He might be ready to get to the point. When they'd shoved all those papers in front of me to sign, I wrote— scrawled over their legalese—NO COLOSTOMY BAG! I don't even like hearing them use the word colon. I'm sick, but that makes me sicker.

So they were supposed to just knock me out and get in there and see what's really up. He takes a step closer, puts his palm on my knee. Oh, boy.

"We did not fix anything or remove anything. We always have to weigh—"

The arrogant nurse interrupts him to say he may need to put things quite simply.

"You had to weigh something? You just told me you didn't remove anything."

"We always have to weigh a recovery interval against presumed life expectancy." Now he retreats to silence.

He wants me to react. What a jerk. Do they teach them that? Just stand there in your ostentatious, blindingly white lab coat and don't say another word?

"Where's that juice I heard so much about?"

He gives a half-hearted glance over his shoulder, pretends he's looking for the juice. Then back at me, tucks the chin, wrinkles the forehead. Very Hollywood.

"How about my clothes?" Oh, they're on a chair over there. Thing is, they're mine. Not like anything else here. Not even the warm blanket that isn't warm anymore.

The forsaken little rail yard I'm standing above, home to a couple dozen hardy souls of scant means, lies adjacent to the abandoned mill it used to serve. There's an ongoing dispute over who owns the yard property—a real Who's Who of creditors. There's also a challenge to how the recent rezoning *slipped like a mouse through a hole in the baseboard*, according to our local newspaper, right out of the town council chamber and right into the ordinance book.

Right-of-ways and easements are peculiar, it seems, complicated enough to make your head spin unless you're a lawyer, in which case, they make your billables clock spin. Bankrupted receivership, who had been paying to insure the yard, who quit paying? No insurer will touch it now before ownership is settled.

So nothing will happen to this squatter community until someone in the circular firing squad at the courthouse has been declared Last One Standing. The eviction process at the rail yard would not even *start* until then. That's what my new acquaintances—who have apparently made quite fine neighbors of themselves here by the tracks—have told me, and some of them have been through this very sort of uncertainty in their past.

I see how they focus on and help each other, but with no urgency. Less anyway than I see every day in the unabashedly individual, mostly self-serving endeavors that bustle through the town behind me, my own stomping ground.

I got busy on a list, two actually. Everything I own is now on there somewhere. Into the first column went all my nice-to-have items that are small enough for a hypothetical pedestrian to transport and are, together, small enough to fit in the storage unit I just rented in town. Any item not in the first column is in the second: SELL OR GOODWILL'S.

Half of us drive. Twice a day we empty the toilet—the five-gallon bucket. I'm not saying where, because we need those places. Crazy thing to need, but there you are. Just about anything anybody anywhere needs, though, is crazy in its own way. One might not realize that yet like I do.

So the cars…we tend to team up, though there's no rule about it. If there were, it would be One Car Per Pair. Me, I haven't paired up yet, but I want to pretty soon, because things are already getting steadily harder like the surgeon with the mole—the Ghost of Saint Hospital—told me they would.

I took the pills faithfully till I gave up my rented house and then kept taking them a couple of more weeks here at The Yard. Till I got adjusted, a month ago. Now I have to hold some money back for food and gasoline. I fetch a lot of our water from town too. Good citizenship. You know, I keep telling myself, go ahead and be a burden sometimes, when you must, just don't turn into a pain in the ass.

Dewayne says he likes my twelve-year-old Chrysler 300 because he would be able to fit lying down in the back seat. He's happy-go-lucky and all but he whistles a lot. Loud. Sometimes I think, alright, I could get a cot that spans the console and sleep in front. Some folks here have one of those. But I do cry out in pain several times every night, and how would that be? Makes whistling all day seem not so bad. His whistling *is* kind of bad, though. What grates— I finally figured out—is its intent, that those shrill outbursts are voluntary. Unlike my shrieks, which, to their credit, shoot out of me like a comet. A ball of agony with a tapering tail of good old-fashioned fear. So no.

Linda Q is looking to pair up too. We've got only five women in the whole yard, and she pretty much despises the other four. Here she comes.

"Danner, gimme a ride. I need some lady kind of things and a few boxes of ramen."

She smells good, always, not like any of the rest of us. I suppose in an office building, that fact would stand out to only some of the people, but here, everybody notices. I'll drive her, sure, like I have before. She's about sixty, warm round face, and that's another thing we all notice. You could do worse for a partner, so I think somebody will be grateful to get paired with her.

"I'm meditating," I tell her. Part playful put-off, part true. "Time to pair up, just don't know who." My true part.

Linda says, "The Bekins guy my daughter hired to haul away all my furniture? He told me, *Take your time about pairing up,* if I came here. *You got to watch and listen.*"

"If I had time."

She *knows* I don't.

Last week I signed over my car. When I did I felt different, better. Others kept asking me, did I get good news from the doctor? Was someone coming to visit me? No, I just wanted somebody to be able to own it after me.

Only a few days later though, Rolly announced that I wasn't allowed to sleep in my old car anymore. It was his. Well—what's next was not my idea and I voted against it—we did drag him behind the mill and do very bad things to him. Guess I should've *watched and listened* better before giving it away. I didn't do the bad things but I was there. So now screw the title. I'll just make it well known around camp who the next owner will be. But somebody's always got to go and wreck something good. I didn't expect that here.

"Linda, I don't want to pair up with you, but you can visit any old time. Ready for town?"

"Rettie."

We park our cars next to each other, my partner Hal and me, near the rail switch. No one wanted the spot. Some said it was unlucky. The thought is that this was where a particular freight car and another and another made their final switch before leaving The Yard forever.

The thought couldn't bother me less. I said to Hal that, whenever that was happening, the railcar could look back and think how it had been the center of attention at the moment it switched rails. And that, when it left the switch behind, a new existence somewhere else could begin. And what's so bad about that?

Good that I didn't wait longer to partner up. So much for watching and listening. I had been too busy lately watching myself stumble, double over, and listening to myself not finish sentences, lose track. Plus Hal had helped me get to the bucket more than a few times.

Hal's going on about his son and his son's family, how great their life is. I never talk about mine—they've all been gone for so long, I truly don't think about them and would have to struggle to come up with a few good things if I did. But see, this pleases me. To not talk about them. To make the right decision to not talk. Like how I made the right decision to get rid of all my big things and move to The Yard. To not be alone.

"They're about as perfect as I ever wished my folks' family was, when I was growing up," Hal says.

He's squinting. With that wiry frame of his, he's able to squat quite low, but the smoke from our dinner fire is wafting into his eyes anyway. I hear little grunts that tell me he's proud of cooking. It's some kind of pork thing on our long skewer, and he's stubborn about burning off all the grease.

I kind of want to ask him, *Oh yeah? Well, where's this hotshot son of yours this minute, while his admiring father soldiers on, day after long day in the rail yard?*

But I'm not going to say that, not today. And not tomorrow, in case there is one for me. Everyone is aware that the storage key is always in the front-left pocket of my jeans, along with the list. When Hal and I are done eating,

I'll add the few remaining names, who to give what to. I think I finally know by now.

They Mostly Have Faces

"They're not straight," says Agnes, from her bed closer to the window. The blinds in fact are crooked. I must bring this up with Tim when we talk. Why allow the possibility of torment here? When we've reached the point where our bodies at last have gone to hell but our minds haven't yet, can't we be granted a humane degree of simple order to keep those minds safe against constant aggravation?

Which is what my own mind has been experiencing since a few minutes ago, when Hutchie tore the Mickey D's bag from my grip before I could make it to Mom's room. So I had to give Mom the Big Fuckin' Mac in a bag whose top was torn off, because of course there's no reason I should ever be able to get all the way down the hall bearing the bright attitude I bore when I entered the lobby.

But Mom doesn't mind. She lets the now empty bag float to the floor, where I intend to let it stay, in the dim hope the staff may learn from this artifact, if they happen to pair it with what Hutchie dropped next to her left wheel.

Wheelchairs are the optimal elevation for causing and recovering a McDonald's fumble. They also cover a lot of ground, notwithstanding the short reach of these patients' arms. And the good folks play zone here, not man to man.

In a different twist, North Dakota—I was once told—is a place where the residents toss their trash to the plains just to give the landscape some color and contour. And that reminds me of another twist on trash, all the way back to when I was in law school in Chicago. On a trip to one of Al Capone's hangouts on the Fox River, we inadvertently toured the community of Valley View, whose residents' ancestors won their land through a newspaper contest. The descendants decorate their lots, and especially the vacant lots in the hills and crotches, with only very large unwanted items like refrigerators, stoves, air conditioners, and don't forget cars. Jim-Bob, did you dump the car yet? Which one?

So I guess no one is learning from trash, not even the folks of North Dakota. People who aren't from there don't go there. So the communities are not swimming in tourist tax dollars. And the litterbugs still wonder why.

Mom is grinning while she chews, looking like a clown who forgot to paint her face. And I am back to the place I was in when the big door to the lobby swung itself open for me. At peace. Maybe I won't pester Tim about the blinds after all. And Agnes is at peace too, and not trying to climb down to the floor and pilfer the burger.

Driving home, I'm remembering last night's dream, in which I was writing a brief to sue the nursing home over the quality of their food. I had somehow convinced the partners to let me file. Of course, in the same dream, George W. Bush declined to shake my hand at a house party. He did smile, though.

Any of us will acknowledge that our beloved Paducah is best known for the perpetually high number of escaped prisoners still on the lam—federal from Marion in Illinois and county from our McCracken—and for how abysmal our nursing homes truly are. Either can keep you up at night. I've got to laugh, though, at the thought that the single type of domicile safe from break-ins by escapees is the nursing home.

You wouldn't go there to shelter. You go there to die.

It's such a nice Sunday, I zip into the roadhouse lot on Hinkleville Road to grab a seat at one of the tables on their covered patio and to tap out a few thoughts there about my pending case. I already know flies are not bad here. Left hand on the door latch of the Bimmer, right hand on the laptop strap, let's get that ice cold beer.

The job: to decide upon the value of the woman's eye she lost at the plant. There's a lot to consider, and I'm good at this. The partners like to throw me the heartbreaking cases because, okay, I am sentimental. They've caught me in tears a couple of times at my desk. My craft is in getting the plaintiff to start telling the jury about the many ways their lives have been stripped of little joys and, in some cases, of love itself. This then, also, can keep *me* up at night.

The young lady with the note pad—Bridgie, her badge says—is new. I've never seen her here, and she tells me she is. Been here only three weeks. In town only ten months. She doesn't speak Server.

Bridgie brings out my brew, and I'm surprised that, when I tap the chair next to mine, she sits. She smiles crooked, her left end higher. "What're you working on?" she wants to know.

I tell her about the eye. "I wish I could say this was the first eye from that place." I go on a little to tell her what the research is like and how many things I'll make the jury weigh.

Bridgie interrupts. "And there's the other thing…not just how awful life is now, but also what it was like when it first happened. I mean…was it hanging down out of the socket? See, then she wouldn't know whether to grab it and should she take the time to wash her hands first."

She speaks Early Twenties. But she doesn't speak Kentucky. Maybe Illinois. Except for the piercing at her brow, which I at fifty-three find regrettable, her manner is at once naïve and unashamed. A sprawl of ash blonde is swirling above and around her pretty face after an apparent attempt to tie it back. But I'm listening to an empathetic soul.

"And what it felt like," she continues, "when she did grab it for the ride to the hospital. Was all the pain in her socket, or did the eyeball in her hand hurt? Plus, where'd she go? Lourdes?"

"Why?"

"I'm just picturing her walking into their ER."

The whopping May thunderboomer I'd heard about was hurtling toward the house by the time I slipped the Bimmer into the garage. I made quickly for my windowless den at the core of the house. A power outage was reasonable to expect out here, where so much wiring is overground. That's what all the candles in the den are for.

I really want to make notations of the many thoughts Bridgie raised. Not that I'd fail to think of those, but I want to remember her *tone of voice* as she spoke each of them. There was such serendipity in this encounter that I'd be already telling my wife about, if she weren't the wife I don't have anymore.

So the whiteboard and I bulletize the list of Bridgie's concerns. This keeps me from getting so involved with one that something about another escapes to the ether. Now I can elaborate the hell out of each of them, and I will.

The electricity survived. Glory be. I'm tapping in the last few thoughts when Mom calls. To say thanks again for the Big Mac, I suppose.

But no. "Are you missing anything, Roger? Think. Remember showing me the storm radar?"

"My iPad."

"I figured I'd better let you know now, in case you'll need it for work tomorrow."

And actually, I do, so I tell her I'll be leaving soon to get back there and pick it up. Would she like anything in particular to brighten her evening? A trashy romance novel, perhaps, for being such a good girl?

I swung into the truck stop to get that novel for Mom and found a little crystal owl fetish for Bridgie for having been so wise, so aware.

When I get back on Hinkleville Road, I realize this is déjà vu in reverse. But that's okay. I'll take a different route home after I pick up the iPad.

I find Bridgie on the vacated patio. *On* the concrete. She tells me in gasps that she was toting the tray full of empties and got lightheaded. The bottles and mugs started to teeter and fall and so, in an uncalculated maneuver, she tried to get low to mitigate the damage. That's how she twisted her right leg, the one that is throbbing like a toothache.

"Lourdes?" I ask her.

"Please."

"I'll get your purse. Where is it?"

I fetch her a wheelchair from the ER. The place is full of wounded weekend warriors and druggies, but a quick chat with a nurse bumps Bridgie up in the queue.

She doesn't have insurance and she won't be able to afford the medical bills, let alone the physical therapy. And she's got nobody local. But she won't sue the roadhouse for her own mistake. She's too good a person.

I haven't told her yet. I'm going to cover her bills. I just will.

We're more than two hours in now. Mom has tried to call twice. I'll call her when they wheel Bridgie in. No, when I've taken her home.

"You're really not gonna pick up?" Bridgie says.

"Later."

Bridgie buries her head in my shoulder again.

This time I kiss her hair. *She's not your daughter. She's not your daughter. I know, I know.* "I have something for you. Don't let me forget."

"I have no idea what that means," she says, through a wince.

"There's your iPad. The chair by the door."

But I'm already headed for Mom's little dresser. "I'm going to brush your hair."

"You're going to be late for work."

"Yes, I'm going to brush your hair *and* I'm going to be late for work. Turn your head *that* way."

It's easier than I thought. We've got tangles, but they're giving up.

"How is your little friend?" Mom asks.

"She's not little, she's young. And alone. Moved here from Peoria with a boyfriend who turned out to be the devil. The guy grew up in Paducah. More later, but for now…" I clear my throat, twice, as a sort of vocal drum roll. "Deep in the caverns," I whisper, "of Cave In Rock Park…" The rhyme she used to recite to me when she'd brush my hair. The rhyme she had written for me. "Deep where few ever tread, lay / A little boy huddled alone in the dark / Stunned, in his hunger and dread. // Along came his mother with help from a friend / Searching up high and down low / Pausing to pray, now and again, for / Guidance of where to go."

"Oh, Roger. I can't believe you remember that."

"That sounds lovely," Agnes pitches in, "but why can't you speak up?"

"This boy did by luck hear her desperate calls / As she, in turn, heard his cries / Their voices resounded off slippery stone walls. / The flashlight beam troubled his eyes. // Aw, Mom, that's as far as I can go." I lied. I just want to hear the last stanza in *her* voice. "Can you finish it?"

"She knelt in the puddle in which he had lain."

"Yeah!"

"And thanked the Good Lord for her son. / He poked at her arm so hard it caused pain, and / Said that he just…wants…to…run!"

"I guess I do have to run. Miss Agnes, please, as needed, assure my dear mother that I am not in fact dating a twenty-two-year-old? Mom, listen to Agnes. I'll call you tonight."

Before I could call her, Mom called me about the problem at the home and tripped on her words a few times as the urgency grew. It was a plumbing thing.

"Roger, the faucet runs and runs. It gushes. I won't be able to sleep tonight."

"Hand your phone to Agnes."

"Oh, I can't. She's gone."

"Then call me again when she comes back." Clever on my part.

Clever until Mom tells me Agnes isn't coming back. "They took her away."

"Why, and where to?"

"Tim says they want her to be safe."

I say I gotta go. I call Tim. Ask him why he hasn't called me and I tell him not to move a goddamned inch.

A couple seconds after the Bimmer has nosed itself into the parking lot, the wife I don't have anymore is whispering into my head. *You're just here to gather information. Don't go and be your jerk lawyer self.*

Tim has got a steaming paper cup in his left hand and he's tugging at his beard with the other. He's leaning so hard against his office door frame that, if it were to suddenly cave, he'd be on his ass. He looks altogether too casual waving me in.

In as placid an information-gathering tone as I can muster, I ask him, "Did you fix the faucet yet? And how long has it been leaking?"

"Roger," he says, "let's sit. How much time do you have?"

I nod.

"We can talk?" Tim tells me there never was a leak. There never was a gushing sound. That this happens. That it's to be acknowledged but not to invoke panic. That Mom has had a few delusions, and among other things, they're concerned about the frequency, how many days between, and whether there's any attendant physical risk to the patient or those around her. This was the case this evening. Hence, they've moved Agnes to a vacant bed in another room. "Only to mitigate risk." Mom did, after all, shove Agnes, who had wrapped her arm around Mom to try to calm her.

When he was almost done telling me these things, my phone gonged with a fresh text. I stole a glance. It's from Bridgie, and she's telling me thanks again for everything I did and that she's beginning to feel better and is wishing the best for me. Maybe I'll respond, maybe not, but not now.

I'm going to walk down the hall and talk to Mom, I tell Tim. "Not that I don't believe you."

"Roger, I've had her sedated. She's out. We'll see where she's at after a good night's sleep. I'll shoot you a text in the morning, either way. I promise."

I want to blame the home. I want to blame Tim. I'm not certain I don't want to blame Agnes too, but I picture her having to adjust to a new room and a new roommate, just for having tried to be of comfort to my mom.

I rise, lost in these thoughts. "Did you at least give Agnes a bed by a window?"

Voices, thoughts, doubts. I want to pass the time in near darkness, so I light only two of the candles in the den. Only the hood light illuminates the kitchen. The four fingers of Evan Williams in my cut crystal tumbler, purposed for sedation, will help. That and its sparkle.

Warm cockles are starting to ease my consciousness. The sweetness of my stranger from Peoria intrudes and stirs me, so I do place a call to her, and she picks up rather quickly. But that probably makes sense, given that she'd have the phone very near, not risking a sudden move on that right leg.

I don't know, we sound like two persons who know each other but have never spoken to one another over the phone. The ragged handoffs are a matter of timing and anticipation, I suppose. I resolve to get more rhythmic for my part.

I also resolve to not tell Bridgie about Mom's episode. Perhaps this is a *Cast not your pearls before swine* premonition, that I don't want the vision of my mom, she struggling so much, to be *trampled* by this innocent listener, who surely would try to understand before failing to.

"I hope my text didn't come at a bad time for you," Bridgie says.

"Not at all. I just couldn't respond right away. Something came up about my mother. Tell me about you."

"I heard from the radiologist. From Lourdes? He was looking at the ultrasound report. He said they read it wrong, the technician. The MRI showed the MCL is sprained. It's…not…torn! So he said just wear the immobilizer, except in bed, and see how it goes. I can put weight on it and walk, *if* it doesn't hurt too much. Roger, I want to go back to work!"

"Bridgie. There's Worker's Comp, and I could help with that. And if the roadhouse isn't insured for WC, then, with today's news, we can assume your future bills will be finite and affordable for them. This is such good news, in every way. But you should rest and be cautious. And I haven't even figured out a way to get your car to you."

"But can't you see? That's not a problem if you can take me to work tomorrow."

I'm perturbed now. This fathering business will require patience. "Not tomorrow."

"But I'm putting some weight on it. As in…one foot in front of the other? Short steps, but hey. It doesn't hurt with the thing on."

"You may not have discovered this yet, Bridgie, but restaurants invented wet floors. If you slip, you may mess that leg up for the rest of your life. If you want encouragement to go back to work, you won't get it from me."

"Tell me about Mom."

I hate this. Why can't we talk about one thing at a time? But I do see a window to settle my own nerves. And I spill the story. At first in measured droplets. Then, I guess you could say, I let it gush. "And there are other instances, and I don't know what those feature. Maybe not water. I'll find out some things in the morning."

"Could you get her one of those electric waterfall things, over rocks, where she could drip some essential oil in the water and get herself chill? Or…one of those machines that makes white noise? So she can hear more of that and less of that stupid faucet."

I was able to persuade the clerk from our office to ride with me to the roadhouse and follow me as I drive Bridgie's car to her apartment. She was getting the car back on my condition that she not drive just because she's feeling her oats. And I finally gave Bridgie the owl. "To commemorate your wisdom."

"You want me to be wise," she said, "and not drive."

"No. I got this for you because you *were* wise, in your thoughts about the blinded woman. But…continuing to be wise *would* be good."

Now, two weeks later, the days that have passed have redefined drama to me. The eye case was first and foremost until Mom's episodes became first and foremost until dissuading Bridgie from going back to work too soon became first and foremost. I've finished the voir dire and my final preps for the eye trial. But Mom has had more dalliances in the unreal.

The crooked blinds across the window were now an old TV to Mom, one that she screamed she needed someone to fix. "See? The lines across the picture?" She's old enough to recall a repairman performing horizontal convergence adjustments from behind the console while she held a mirror for him, in front of it. "Why can't someone bring me a mirror?"

My visit found her wobbling at her walker in the hall, possibly drugged up. I carried her back to bed.

"Goddamnit, Tim."

"We *can* restrain her, Roger. That in itself can be quite frightening, though. We're working to pinpoint just the right dosage."

Had this not come on a day when Bridgie told me she has gone back to work and that "It was pretty scary," I may have been able to be my lawyerly self. But no. That character may no longer exist in my personal life.

So, six fingers. One candle.

Just when there was so little to celebrate, the jury award was sufficiently generous to surprise even me. My client's husband and her son jumped out of their seats and over the rail and tried to pull my arms out. She took my hand and squeezed the blood out of it while a stream of tears poured from her uncovered eye.

Two fingers and four candles later, I knew. I knew what I wanted to do. It involved crappies, blackening spice, red potatoes, yellow onions. And butter butter butter.

"No pressure," I said, "but tell me your days off for next week."

Bridgie did.

"Then Monday, I'm going to rent a small RV and a small aluminum motorboat on a trailer and head to Lake Barkley; come back Tuesday morning, maybe with a cooler full of crappies!"

"They kind of got me, Roger."

"Who?"

"The authorities. I'm on recognizance."

"I'll be right there."

Turns out, there was no devil boyfriend. There was a not insignificant shoplifting charge in Peoria. Paducah had been a stop to pee, but it already felt more comfortable than Marion, since, by unconsidered logic, Marion would be less safe by way of being in the state in which the crime had taken place. She had been arraigned in Peoria, but fled trial.

"I was going to call you and ask would you be my lawyer. Today. I was."

"But Bridgie, I don't do criminal law. How did you convince the judge, now, that you're not a flight risk? I mean, that's almost automatic."

"I showed him my knee. I took the thing off. And I told him I can't drive—no way and that's why I missed so much work. And I said I don't know anyone except for a kind lawyer."

"When is the extradition hearing?"

"Friday next week."

"Pack an overnight bag for Monday."

We did fairly well on the lake, despite that rain had been likely and that, when some fish sense this, they float eerily patient for the worms and bugs that would flood in from shore when it does rain. Why help yourself to a snack when you can wait for a buffet?

When I eased the first crappie down into the water of the live net bag, Bridgie grabbed my forearm and said, "You find something really good and you take it, and then you're swept away." She shook her head fast, appearing to hope this thought would fall out of it. "Just for trying to stay alive."

I took her hand, glided my thumb across her knuckles.

She said, "Don't you think people should be able to do whatever they have to do to stay alive?"

"I did think that, when I was doing pro bono in Chicago. I'm maybe jaded now. Anyway, I thought you were talking about the fish."

"I was. But it reminded me of me."

"What did you hope you would become? Grown up."

"A vet. Veterinarian."

"Why?"

"I think because they mostly have faces. The animals? Just like me."

"My ex-wife has a face. I swear, there's nothing endearing about hers anymore."

Bridgie's eyes were damp now. "You have a face," she said, "and I see into you."

By the end of our time on the lake, four not-at-all-bottomish channel cats and three quite large crappies had taken the hook. I dispatched Bridgie to the outhouse after she sucked down a couple quick beers on land. Then I clobbered the cats and filleted the crappies.

I had those puppies in foil, with the taters and onions, before she cautiously hobbled back to the site. I let it be her job to place the foils on the campfire and to make a little foil ashtray for us to drop our pickers into, so we wouldn't attract overnight skunks.

But we ate in the RV after all. We each enjoyed our exquisite dinner before what should've been a nice light conversation. It was I, though, who brought that down.

"Have you ever been in trouble with the law before this?"

She said there was the matter of her having taken money from the till where she worked when she was twenty. That there was something about her needing to stay clean.

I excused myself and stepped outside next to the fire to call Casco, who practices criminal, to see whether he would be free on Thursday and Friday. He said yes. This will help.

She asked—and I should have known this was coming—how my mom was doing.

"How 'bout let's go outside," I said, "and can I have one of your cigarettes?" I told her about the French-looking columns in the lobby. Added a few remarks about Tim's puffed-up sense of professionalism. But there *was* more trouble, I told her. Not such wild delusions lately, but she has been kicking other patients under the table in the dining hall.

Bridgie said, "Oh, that's sad."

"Sometimes I take her fast food. It's tastier than the bland stuff they serve at the home. I should start to do that more often, y'know? Keep her out of their dining hall? Do I know *your* story, Bridgie? Do I know it now?"

"Everything, Roger. Just not the stillborn."

I hushed the MP3. "You have something in common with my mother."

"Aw."

"I don't imagine you'll be sticking around," I said. "Would you write to me? After you get settled?"

"I don't know your address."

"True. I'll give it to you when I take you home."

I excused myself, said goodnight, and we slipped quietly into the RV. I had given Bridgie the aft bed and claimed the fore loft bed for myself. It was time to climb up. Bridgie said she was going out for another smoke and she'd hang by the embers for a while. I said, "Hold that railing when you're hopping down."

Then the last thing I remember was turning over to tune out. Sleep came so easy, and I made it through till dawn. Having someone in proximity to care for has reinstalled my elusive tranquility. It has rebooted me.

This morning there's a note on the counter saying simply *I'm sorry Roger.* Should I hitch up and cover some miles along 134? It is the only way.

But she may have—quite likely has—thumbed a ride that would be impossible to catch up to. And that was just as likely to have happened last night as this morning. The *thing*, the immobilizer, may lie in a ditch. I'm deciding to *not* try to find her.

I'll fix myself a nice breakfast. Get back to civilization. Return the rentals, drive home, get showered up, do a half day's work. And go see Mom after her dinner hour.

Then maybe I could stay out of the den later. Wouldn't that be nice?

Tim is in the lobby with some other folks but breaks away from them long enough to say, "She's having a good day, Roger."

And, dog my cats, she is. She gives me a bear hug. And she thanks me for having the pulled pork sandwich and the onion rings and sweet tea delivered. On her nightstand is an empty bag with the roadhouse's name and logo emblazoned. "It was so delicious," Mom says.

"Yes, Mom." I tap her in the triceps. "I suppose it was."

"And that pretty blonde girl was so sweet. It's a shame she had to leave so fast. She practically *ran* out of here—I had to holler not to knock anybody over—but I'm sure she had other deliveries."

"They're gone, just like that, aren't they? Yes, I'm sure she had to hurry to get to the next place she was going. But listen. I'm not the one who ordered that food for you tonight. Maybe you have a secret admirer. Here. In this fine building. I guess all you can do is be grateful for everyone. Grateful and nice as pie. Because we just never, never know."

Mom hands me her brush. "They could be heroes?" She slides down. Her stockinged feet slap the floor in a somewhat military march. "I need you to bring me my luggage."

"Where are you going?"

"That doesn't matter! Look, I know you're a runner, Roger. Promise you won't run, when you're old like me."

"I won't run, Mom. I promise. I'll call for my luggage like you just did." I pull the brush through her bangs.

The clown is back.

Acknowledgements

The following persons have provided careful and honest criticism of stories that appear in this collection. I will always be deeply grateful to them.

The Julia Group, including the brilliant and meticulous Mike Cobb, the epic story crafter Julia Sennette, the late emphatic poet John S. Edwards, the passionate memoirist and adroit artist Dru Sumner, and the tirelessly curious and creative John Ripma.

Blue Ridge Mountains Poets and Writers Guild, including Kathy Williams, Pam Rauber, Mary Encinias, the author pdmac, and the late Rita Kate VanOrsdal.

Batavia Public Library Writers Workshop, including the late spoken-word poet Frank Rutledge, Ray Ziemer, and Kevin Moriarity.

Waterline Writers, including Anne Veague and Kevin Moriarity.

Oswego-Mongomery Branch writers, including Jim Cherry and Andie Schweda.

Robert W. Rowe Wordsmiths, including Melissa Oxborrow, Samantha Brown, and Patricia Ribolzi.

Plano Writers Group, including Jeanne Valentine, Paul Block, Reverend Dave Dean, Rania Zeithar, Vivian Wright, Laurie O'Connor Stephans, Carl Armstrong, Pat Comer, Rose Walter, Bobby Yarbrough, Stacy Christian, the late poet William James Robertson III, and Reverend Kent Svendsen.

My college Creative Writing professor, Dr. Loren Wilkinson, whom I credit for my lifelong fascination in the short story art form.

And dear friends, including Rebecca Satterfield, Do Cooke, Karen Nasti, and the late Dan Finn, who loved to read my work and contributed astute comments.

About the Author

Glen Heefner fondly recalls nights in his college days when he and another student would take a drive to the lake, where they would climb down the steep bluff to the shore. They'd gather driftwood for an unabashed campfire and spend hours talking of nothing but literature. Then, on some Saturdays, he would hop a train for the hour-long ride to the city, where the big bookstores would send him back to campus with another armload of short story collections and anthologies.

One day Heefner would write short stories of his own. This was a perennial promise he made to several of his closest friends, who must have always thought, tongue in cheek, *Sure you will.*

Only five years before retiring from his 23-year career in technical writing did he begin to do that. He's been making up for lost time.

Glen lives in the mountains of North Georgia.

Glen Heefner